KANSAS TRAIL

After the Civil War ruined his life, Bennett Kell threw in his lot with a gang of thievin' guntoughs who rode the Texas–Kansas border. But there was one thing he couldn't steal—fact was, Ada McKittridge had stolen his heart. But to win her hand, Bennett had to strike a deal with her connivin' railroad baron uncle; find a herd of beeves in Texas and drive them up to Kansas City—smack through the blood-soaked territory of the border gangs whose deadly raids had darn near closed down the railroad.

If Bennett survived, Ada was his. He was ready for the challenge but faced tough times ahead . . .

Hascal Giles was born in Big Stone Gap, Virginia on July 30, 1922. He was educated in public schools in Big Stone Gap. His first job was as a sports writer for the *Kingsport Times-News* in 1942. Giles began writing primarily Western short fiction for pulp magazines in the wee hours of the morning once the newspaper was put to bed. He became serious about his pulp writing but was no less serious about his career as a newspaperman. In 1948 he decided to try his hand at making a living freelancing. Giles started writing feature novelettes for Range Riders Western and Masked Rider Western and began expanding his pulp novelettes into novels that he sold to lending library publishers such as Arcadia House. *Kansas Trail* (1956) was his first original novel for Ballantine Books. Over the years other novels appeared, like *Texas Maverick* (1990) *Texas Blood* (1992). They are stories imbued with moral dilemmas, emotional suffering, and the achievement of wisdom as the result of extraordinary, even shattering, confrontations with the best and worst in human nature. The dominating themes of his fiction are the twisted tapestry of the past revealed in the present through the harsh light of psychological revelation, the examination of the false premises and moral weaknesses that produce so much anguish and misfortune in life, the explosive sexual aspect of the love a man and a woman can have for each other, the importance of family and love, and the ultimate need to be able to forgive and to learn from conflict. They are themes that will long retain their intense relevance and also reward the interest of anyone who happens to come upon a story carrying his byline.

KANSAS TRAIL

Hascal Giles

GUNSMOKE

This hardback edition 2008
by BBC Audiobooks Ltd
by arrangement with
Golden West Literary Agency

ISBN 978 1 405 68191 9

British Library Cataloguing in Publication Data available.

Printed and bound in Great Britain by
Antony Rowe Ltd., Chippenham, Wiltshire

One

Coming down the slope of the wooded ridge, Bennett Kell rode with his ears tuned to the sounds about him—to the cawing of crows in a thicket above him, to the whisper of the hot breeze through the aspens bordering the creek below; and to the occasional hoofbeats behind him.

The rider had been following him for nearly an hour. Far back on the trail a hoof striking against stone had warned him, and he had been alert ever since. Twice he had changed course but the hoofbeats had stayed with him and now he was sure the rider was behind him for a reason. But there had been no place to stop until now, no place to make a stand without warning his pursuer.

Bennett rode with his eyes straight ahead, outwardly calm, although his nerves were quivering. In this moment there seemed to be a warning to Bennett Kell to get out of this land before he died here. He wanted to get out, had considered it for weeks; now he might not get another chance. . . .

With an effort he held the horse to a steady gait. At

the bottom of the hill he forded the shallow stream and reined his dun into a thick screen of aspen and box elder. Patting the horse reassuringly, he lifted his rifle from the saddle boot and sat with the gun cradled in the crook of his arm while he watched his back trail.

The other man was good at his job. He had circled the girth of the hill, and Bennett did not see him until he appeared at the opposite side of the stream, twenty yards away. He paused there a moment, his eyes searching the aspen. As he lifted the reins to come on, Bennett sidestepped the dun into view and said, "That's far enough, Rusk."

Startled, Toby Rusk stood in the stirrups, his hand sliding toward the gun on his hip. Then he relaxed, settling both hands on the pommel.

"Getting kind of bossy, ain't you, Bennett?" Rusk's anger was genuine: he hadn't wanted to get caught at this.

"You can take it that way," Bennett told him shortly. "But mostly I'm just cautious. There's been a shakeup in the railroad shipping set-up. Thayer's been tossed out and a man named McKittridge is taking over. He's one of the big muckety-mucks and I don't want somebody like you messing up the deal. You're supposed to be with the others, so get back there."

His words were deliberately blunt. They suited their target and his own surly mood. The sight of Toby Rusk, big and brawny and stinking with stale sweat, always angered him.

Raising a thick hand, Rusk cuffed back the brim of his ragged hat. "It ain't McKittridge that's bothering you, Bennett. It's something else. You keep to yourself too much, like the rest of us have got lice. Why don't

6

you spit it out? That's what I tagged along to find out. You mosey around by yourself like you was hiding something from us. Why don't you own up to it? Then I'll go back."

"You'll go back anyway," Bennett said flatly. "It looks as if you want to boss this outfit."

"That's exactly what I want. I wouldn't be so easy with my gun, and we'd all be better off." Suddenly Rusk grinned, pleased with his frankness.

"It's not likely to happen while I'm here, Rusk." Bennett shoved the rifle back into the boot, and started the dun slow-walking toward the creek. "I'm coming across. If you want to settle something we'll do it when I get over there. If you don't want a fight you can turn and ride back."

Their eyes met and held, and the dun kept moving. Rusk rubbed his hands along the seams of his greasy buckskin leggings, his mouth pursed thoughtfully. Then, just as the dun's forefeet touched water, Rusk turned his horse and rode away. Over his shoulder he said, "You got a mean look in your eye, Bennett. I don't know how deep it goes. Maybe not very deep. I can wait a while to find out."

Bennett watched the man out of sight, anger and revulsion churning a bitter troth in his mouth. He had hoped Rusk would stand and fight. Sooner or later it had to come, for somehow Rusk sensed that Bennett was working against his conscience, and the big man considered this a weakness.

They were frequently at odds, but Bennett had avoided a showdown with the man simply because he was avoiding a showdown with himself. Somehow the two seemed tied together. It might have come today if

Rusk had not chosen to wait him out a while longer, for Bennett had been ready. He hated the man, and the urge to maul him with his fists grew stronger each day he knew him. But, he told himself honestly, the fight would have accomplished nothing. What he really hated were the things Rusk represented.

And Bennett Kell represented the same things. . . .

Once again he turned the horse. He rubbed a palm across the heavy growth of beard on his face, thinking that he looked no better than Toby Rusk. In a few more years he would have Rusk's thick belly, and the crude speech and swaggering manner.

It was a distasteful prospect, a life foreign to all the things his humble, churchgoing parents had reared him to respect. Bennett Kell had made a mistake in deciding vengeance would heal a wound. He had known this for months now, but he had made no move to remedy the situation. Each time he rode into Kansas City he promised himself it would be the last, but he kept coming back again and again. He rode on, calling himself less than a man because he could find no turning point.

Bennett Kell met McKittridge in a steaming board shack beside the new rails which had come spearing from the East into Kansas City. They talked about cattle, and McKittridge didn't ask too many questions. Bennett liked him for that.

"I'm a railroad man," McKittridge told him, "so I don't know much about cattle. But you probably don't know much about railroads. They're backed by rich men who want to get richer. They get impatient, too.

That's why you don't see Mr. Thayer, our former cattle buyer, around here any more. I'm acting as agent for the packing firms myself."

"So?" Bennett showed as little curiosity as possible. So far the man had given him only cursory attention, talking over his shoulder while he studied a survey map which was spread out on a plank shelf. If McKittridge had shown more than ordinary interest in Bennett's craggy, sun-browned face, Bennett would have turned and left.

"So we've got to show the backers some better results," McKittridge murmured after a moment. "We've got to prove they'll get something back on their investment one of these days."

Bennett merely nodded. McKittridge had the stubborn chin of a cavalry commander and the bright eyes of a dreamer. He dreamed of building an empire, and, Bennett judged, he enjoyed thinking aloud.

"We hope to drive these rails straight to California or meet somebody halfway," McKittridge said. "Washington blows hot and cold on our land subsidy, and so far luck's been against us here in Missouri. You know what that does to our investors. They throw up their hands and want to get out, want their money back."

McKittridge rubbed the back of his neck and sighed. "It all stems from the fact that we're not doing the job that was expected. We've shortened the trail to Texas and the cattle lands, but it isn't reflected in results. Some tables in the East haven't had beef on them since before the war and they're still not getting it. There's your big complaint. Unless cattle shipments pick up, this railroad will fall apart from the inside out. If the cattlemen in Texas are as overstocked on steers and

9

short on cash as they say, you'd think we'd get a trail herd in here every day. Instead, a man like you shows up once a month."

Bennett scowled, wondering if McKittridge was as uninformed as he sounded. Texas men would crawl here with steers on their backs if they could make it, and many had tried the trail.

Bennett said, "You've heard of the border gangs, I guess."

McKittridge's balled fist struck the maps with a clattering sound. "Ah, yes, I've heard of them. Murdering, thieving barbarians left over from the guerrilla bands who tried to fight the war on their own grounds. It's shameful, Kell. Cowards and thieves lying in wait either to extort money from the Texans or steal their herds. We need those cattle."

"I can let you have two hundred head," Bennett said.

McKittridge was glad to get back to business. "Good. The price is fifteen dollars at the loading pens."

Bennett shook his head, a humorless smile twisting his lips. He rubbed a hand across the day-old stubble of black beard on his face and started for the door. "You don't need cattle bad, Mr. McKittridge."

McKittridge grunted. "Make me a price."

"Thirty dollars."

"I'll give you twenty. But I must point out again that I don't know cattle. I assume you do, and I don't expect to be cheated."

"They'll be delivered two days from now at sunup," Bennett said. "I won't be with the herd, so you'll have to meet me somewhere for the payoff. I'll want cash, Mr. McKittridge."

The railroad man nodded. "I have a suite at the

Pioneer House. We could have dinner together, if that's agreeable."

"It's agreeable." He paused on his way out and grinned thinly at McKittridge. "And don't worry. Like you said, I know cattle. They're good Texas steers."

McKittridge gave him a solemn stare. "I doubt that I'll worry much, Kell. I don't know cattle, but I do know men."

The words made Bennett Kell wince. He stepped out quickly into the bright Missouri sunshine, sharply conscious that McKittridge had not asked where the cattle came from.

Two nights later McKittridge answered Bennett's knock at the door in the Pioneer House. McKittridge was a big, florid-faced man with thin gray hair and large, melancholy blue eyes. He wore an expensively tailored black suit which managed to conceal any excessive flesh on his six-foot frame, and he had a habit of rocking gently on his heels when deep in thought.

He rocked now as his glance went over Bennett Kell. Bennett had bathed and shaved carefully for this appointment and he was somewhat amused that McKittridge did not recognize him. With the beard gone, he looked more like himself. He was a tall, lean-waisted man in his middle thirties, although he looked older. His hair was long and dark and despite his efforts with a comb remained shaggy. He had a rider's awkward grace afoot and the plainsman's habit of swinging his dark, piercing eyes over a new scene with swiftness and finality.

The interval at the door lengthened, and Bennett felt

11

impatience prick at him. He slapped his wide-brimmed black hat against the worn knee of his moleskin pants. Aside from the patched and dusty levis he wore when riding, they were all he owned. He was aware that his colorless flannel shirt was drab beside McKittridge's starched whiteness.

"Best I had, Mr. McKittridge," he said smilingly, brushing at his clothes again.

"Pshaw!" McKittridge smiled, recognition flooding his eyes. "I was simply taken aback by the charm you rugged chaps bring with you into a room. I always am. And you needn't feel bad about wearing the gun. I suppose it's a natural habit. Come in, Kell, come in!"

Bennett Kell went in, somewhat abashed. He was learning about McKittridge. The man had a way of keeping another at arm's length, a way of establishing relative positions quickly and subtly. The remark about the gun had done it. Bennett carried a .45 Colt. It rode in an oiled holster low on his right thigh, and above it his slanting shell belt threw off the gleam of brass cartridges. When he walked his fingertips brushed close to the white bone handle, but he was seldom conscious of its being there. Now it felt like a leaden weight dragging at his leg.

He was thinking of the gun when he saw the girl, and he was embarrassed. She came through an arched doorway into the parlor, pausing at sight of the men. Her long golden hair held the glory of a spring sunrise, caught like a jewel against the burgundy draperies over the window. The white ruffles on her pale green dress swirled to embrace a full, mature figure. She had acquired a flawless, creamy tan and Bennett read gen-

12

tleness in her wide gray eyes and warmth in her curving red lips.

McKittridge's eyes lighted, and he stepped across to take her slender left hand in both his own. "This is my niece, Ada McKittridge," he said. "Maybe they'll never give me full credit for holding a railroad in line, but they'll remember me here for bringing the prettiest woman in the world to Missouri. And a sensible girl, too. When we started this thing out here I worried about what I was to do with Ada. We've been together since she was a tot, and there's only the two of us left with the McKittridge name. But when it was time to move there was no problem. Ada wouldn't hear of anything except to come with me. She knows where history is in the making, Kell, and she wants a part of it."

Bennett waited for her to smile. It came, and it filled the room with the radiance he had expected. He nodded and the girl came toward him, her eyes frankly appraising him.

"You know what they say about Big Jim McKittridge, Mr. Kell?" She laughed. "Give him as many as two people for an audience and he'll make a speech. We just happen to add up to that exact number."

Her fingers touched his hand lightly as she took his hat. She had small, soft hands and the touch of them was like a caress. Her gaze met his, as though asking if her nearness pleased him, and then her eyes were veiled by thick lashes as she moved away. Bennett's breath quickened and he felt like a trophy on display as he stood there in the carpeted room with the crystal chandelier gleaming over his head. The Pioneer, with railroad backing and Eastern furnishings, was the most

13

impressive structure in the vicinity of the railroad camp. It had a limited guest list and it catered only to the carriage trade. An invitation from Big Jim McKittridge was the only thing that would ever get Bennett Kell through the front door.

"A fine girl," McKittridge chuckled, dismissing her for the moment. "We'll have a smoke and a chat, Kell, while Ada fusses with the food. I think it's been sent up from the dining room, so it shouldn't take long."

He held out a cigar, and Bennett's impulse was to refuse it. But he changed his mind hastily, accepting the panatela and nodding his thanks. This was a good way to live, he told himself, and a man should partake of it when he could.

They sat on cushioned chairs and smoked for a while, neither speaking. Bennett thought of the nights he had ridden past the Pioneer House on his way to a saloon for a quick drink and a chance to gather information he could turn to profit, never once imagining the kind of people who slept within these walls.

McKittridge's voice broke in upon his thoughts. "I was at the loading pens when the cattle came in today, Kell. They were all you said. Good Texas steers."

Bennett's teeth clamped on the cigar and he sat erect in the chair. McKittridge gave him a sharp glance, and Bennett relaxed outwardly. But his black eyes gleamed with caution.

"I figured you had people to look after the details, Mr. McKittridge."

"That's true. But a man doesn't learn anything behind the scenes, Kell. Sooner or later I look into everything."

Bennett nodded. "A man ought to do that."

14

"Those men who brought the herd in . . . the rough-looking gentleman with the dimples in his cheeks and the slender one with no teeth, in particular. They handled your stock rather crudely. I'm afraid some weight was lost needlessly."

Bennett frowned. The man was doing more than giving information; he was seeking it.

"The dimpled man is Toby Rusk and the toothless one is Wally Bryan." Bennett hid the ghost of a smile behind his cigar. "I may just fire them for that, Mr. McKittridge."

"I'd recommend it," McKittridge said. "You'd do better with Texans like yourself."

"I never said I was from Texas, Mr. McKittridge."

The railroad man smiled. "No, I don't believe you did."

The talk reached a deadlock there. Bennett was aware of it, and it made him uneasy. He had no fear of McKittridge, but he could sense the man's stubborn will. No money had passed between them yet, and McKittridge might simply decide not to pay. Toby Rusk and Wally Bryan had followed him into town, and they'd be expecting their share of the money tonight. They'd be waiting nearby to see that they got it.

The girl's entrance brought a sigh of relief from Bennett. She announced that dinner was served and the three of them went into the dining room. At the doorway McKittridge held back long enough to slip a thick oilskin packet from his inside coat pocket. He handed it to Bennett, a half-smile on his broad face.

"It's all there, and it isn't Confederate scrip, either."

Again Bennett's dark eyes squinted with animal

caution. Then he went on, rebuking himself silently. He was so jumpy he was reading a hidden meaning into every remark his host made.

Ada McKittridge sat directly across from him, and Bennett found it an effort to keep from staring at her. He ate a great amount of fine food without savoring its flavor, and several times he raised his glance to find that the girl was expecting him to look at her. Before they had finished their coffee a knock summoned McKittridge to the door. He returned a moment later and excused himself, explaining that a director of the railroad had arrived unexpectedly. An impromptu conference was being arranged in another room.

As McKittridge hurried out, calling an apology over his shoulder, Bennett fidgeted in his chair. Ada McKittridge refilled his coffee cup and smiled across the table at him.

"That's what you might call a gentle hint, Mr. Kell."

Bennett's hand shook slightly as he stirred the coffee. Ada McKittridge was not brazen or flirtatious, but there was that in her manner which invited him to meet her on the familiar grounds of an established friendship. He wondered vaguely if she was deliberately exciting him with the promise in her eyes so she could laugh at him if he abandoned his judgment and tried to take her in his arms. He discarded the thought at once; she was a puzzling woman, but he was sure she was not that kind.

"I guess a girl like you does get lonesome in these parts," he murmured at last.

"A girl like me, Mr. Kell? I'm like any other girl. We're all at a great disadvantage. We must sit around and wait for someone to ask us to a tea party or a dance or a community social. If no one asks, we just keep sitting. We can't ask them—the men, I mean."

She laughed to show her complaint was one of annoyance and not bitterness. "I wouldn't dare talk like this back in Philadelphia, but I've already learned that folks out here speak their mind and do as they please."

"Not altogether. Nobody does as he pleases, I guess."

Her pretty face grew serious at his earnest tone. "I guess not. But for some reason I decided you did. You have that look about you, as though nothing would stand in the way of what you wanted."

Bennett finished his coffee and stood up. He looked across at her, running his glance over the high breasts and flaring hips, and back to the gold of her hair. "Maybe nothing will," he said softly, and the quick rise of color in her face told him that she did not mistake the meaning of his words.

She came around to walk with him back to the parlor, insisting that he smoke another of her uncle's cigars. Their talk turned to trivial things, of the constant clatter of vehicles in the street and the din of voices and occasional drunken yells which were a part of the throbbing pulse of the growing railhead. She told him of her life in Philadelphia, her nose wrinkling with wry humor when she poked fun at the stodginess of life back East.

"I love this country out here, Mr. Kell," she told him once, and her eyes again met his with that questing, yearning expression she had shown him at dinner. "I want to watch it grow, and to be a part of it. I want my sons to be a part of it."

Time passed quickly, and Bennett was surprised to find himself so pleased by the girl's approval of this

17

rough, raw land of his birth. He told her of the adventures and the challenges offered by life in the West, sharing a sadness with her over the plight of the buffalo and the failure of the white man to learn to live in peace with the Indian tribes.

He was careful to tell her nothing of himself. He wanted to see Ada McKittridge again.

He told her good-by at the door an hour later, and was at the point of asking to see her again when Big Jim McKittridge returned.

Bennett nodded to both of them and fumbled for words. "I'm obliged—" he began, and then sought more adroit language. "I consider it my privilege to be invited here. There's not many folks like you on my back trail. I like the way you live. Some day I aim to do likewise. It was a pleasure."

McKittridge shook hands, nodded, and went toward his bedroom. His back said what he had to say, and Bennett understood the gesture. He could come back here when McKittridge invited him again.

But Ada McKittridge saw the hard twist of Bennett's mouth and she understood that. She stepped outside, closing the door softly behind her.

She took his hands in her own, her face lifted appealingly toward his. "I don't want our friendship to end here, Bennett Kell. I'm sure you know that."

A delicate jasmine scent rose from the gold of her hair and Bennett blamed its heady effect for the churning of his pulse. He said bluntly, "Your uncle would throw me out if I came back here."

"When you're in town, come to the back of the hotel. My window faces the alley. You could make a signal—throw a rock or something."

Bennett smiled, taking an odd thrill from the excitement of her vibrant whispers. "I'll strike three matches. Watch for me a week from tonight."

She nodded and he bent to kiss her, but she gave his hands a quick squeeze and stepped away. Her "Good night" came to him as she went through the door, and he carried the warmth of her voice with him into the night.

The evening had begun for Bennett as a simple business arrangement, but it had evolved into much more than that. He had seen much of poverty and turmoil in his time and little of the orderly prosperity so much in evidence here in the Pioneer House. There were women in his past, women with hard eyes and painted faces whose affection fluctuated with a man's luck. But he had never met one who could stir him so deeply with a glance, or one so obviously pleased to share his company.

The evening at the Pioneer House turned his thoughts back to the course of his own life, making him more certain than ever that it was wrong and wasted. If a man had the daring and self-respect of McKittridge and a woman like Ada to call his own, his life would have purpose and direction.

Bennett Kell meant to have both.

TWO

In the next two months Bennett sold cattle to McKittridge twice. But he was not invited to the hotel suite again. The financial transactions were completed in a bar and McKittridge sent an assistant to handle the business.

Bennett had expected this, so he did not smart under the rebuff. The first invitation had come out of McKittridge's curiosity; with that satisfied, the man kept to his own level.

Still, Bennett gained a devilish satisfaction out of deceiving the man. Employing the signal they had invented that night in the hotel corridor, Bennett and Ada McKittridge met often. But each time he rode into Kansas City he had an uneasy feeling that hidden eyes were watching him; each time he held the girl in his arms he kept expecting McKittridge's deep voice to come out of the night and challenge him.

And now the night had finally come. Bennett had struck the third match and was sitting patiently in the murky alley. An expectant grin spread across his face as footsteps approached the rear door.

The smile faded when he saw the gun. It was aimed at him from the gloom of the hotel corridor. A voice said, "I'd advise you to stand quite still, sir. I fear you've used that rather noticeable signal once too often."

In the challenging voice which barked at him from the darkness there was a note of suppressed anger. Bennett heard it, and his own temper rose defiantly.

He said, "You didn't need to bring a gun, Mr. McKittridge. I'm not going to try to shoot you."

McKittridge swung the door open wider. He wore his usual black suit and the usual determined expression on his heavy-jowled face. "I resorted to a weapon, Kell, because I didn't want you to run away until we talked. I think there's a matter we should discuss at some length."

Through clenched teeth, Bennett said, "Nobody's going to run, Mr. McKittridge. If you're going to lay down some orders you can lay them down here. But you'll have to use that shotgun to make them stick. I'm in love with your niece and I don't figure to be scared away from her unless she does the scaring herself."

McKittridge kept the gun cradled in the crook of his thick arm. "Shall we talk in my suite, Kell? I'll leave the gun here where it belongs."

He stretched and set the shotgun on the wall pegs where it apparently was kept for convenience in the event of a burglary. Then he turned and went up the hallway toward a rear stairway. Bennett followed. It was the only way he could find out how Ada had fared as a result of McKittridge's discovery of their secret courtship.

She was waiting for them in the parlor, and a single

21

glance put Bennett's fears at rest. She was not crest-fallen or burdened by guilt. Instead she looked more radiant and carefree than ever, like a shackled spirit suddenly loosed. She rose smiling at sight of him and walked straight across the room into his arms. Bennett forgot McKittridge's presence and the uncertainty of the moments ahead. He held her close to him, his heart racing as she raised her wide gray eyes to meet his and then lifted her lips to be kissed.

"I love you, Bennett Kell," she whispered in his ear. Then she swung away to look at him with bright lights dancing in her pale eyes, and said it again in a voice that was gay with relief. "I love you, and I don't care if the whole world knows it."

"And you want to marry him, Ada?" McKittridge's voice was a hoarse rumble. He stood with his back against the richly upholstered divan, his hands shoved deep into the pockets of his black coat.

"Yes, Uncle Jim. I know you'd like for him to be a Philadelphia banker or a St. Louis packer, but it doesn't matter. Not really. I think I really came with you out here hoping I'd find a man like Bennett, Uncle Jim. And I've found him."

"This man is a thief and an outlaw, Ada." McKittridge's blue eyes seemed ready to shed tears, but his voice was raw-edged, intent on stripping Bennett Kell of flesh and bone and emotion and laying out a soul for inspection. "You'll find his handiwork along the trails from Texas to Missouri, in unmarked graves and in the bleaching bones of cattle which were slaughtered and stampeded. You've heard of the border gangs, Ada? Meet the boss of one—Bennett Kell."

Ada's eyes widened, and she pressed her fingertips

22

against quivering lips. She stood in stunned silence as McKittridge's voice droned on, indicting Bennett with all the crimes that had been committed by all the bitter men who had come out of the war with a grudge to settle.

Bennett took a step toward the man, fists knotted. His voice came as a rasping, threatening whisper. "You might have let me tell her, McKittridge. I'd have told the truth. At least she'd know I'm not a killer. My men work the hard way—start a stampede, scare off the drivers, then round up the cattle. And we've taken only the leavings. The big boys farther south clean them out first."

McKittridge gave him a disdainful stare. "You've had nearly three months to do it your way, Kell. But Ada tells me she knows nothing of your background. I made it my business to find out."

"But why, Bennett? Why?" Ada's question was a plaintive sound in the still room. "You did tell me about a ranch in Texas. You said you owned it. So why should you steal?"

For a moment he refused to face the girl. He thought of the day Toby Rusk had challenged him on the trail, and of how close he had come to leaving this country forever that day. But then he had met Ada, and had wanted never to leave. He had been afraid to tell her of his purpose here, afraid she would refuse to see him again. He'd been going to ask her to marry him, so they could go back to Texas together, burying his past in Missouri.

He looked at her at last, cringing at the sadness in her eyes. "My old man thought a lot of this country," he said, talking to the girl as though McKittridge were not

23

in the room. "He figured folks like George Washington and Columbus and old Ben Franklin put about as much guts into it as Sam Houston, Davy Crockett or Jeff Davis. So when the war started he figured the Kells ought to stick by them."

"You fought for the Union, Bennett?" Ada came to his side, slipping her arm under his.

He nodded. "When it was over, I went back home, down in the Brazos country. My folks had died and I found out nobody came to their funeral but the preacher. That was because I was fighting with the Yankees. I tried to get the place going again, but nobody would trust me for wages because I fought with the Yankees. That galled me. When somebody tried to burn me out, I ran out of patience. I heard the railroad was building into Missouri and I heard the fellers along the border meant to settle some of their grudge against the Rebs by helping themselves to some Texas beef. So I figured I had a grudge, too."

McKittridge made a clucking sound with his lips. "That's what an angry boy would do, Kell. Come up here to get even. A man would have done otherwise."

"Like what?" Bennett asked angrily.

"Like putting up another fight for his country and doing something that would help people today and for generations to come. You could have helped to put Texas on its feet, Kell, and helped tie this country together with a railroad that will make it grow stronger and richer than any nation on earth."

Bennett's dark eyes glowed with suspicion. "You're making yourself plain now, Mr. McKittridge. You figure the border gangs are going to put the railroad out of business and you're crying over it. What could I do about it?"

"Bring a herd to Missouri." McKittridge faced him, hands jammed hard into his coat pockets, his chin jutting stubbornly. "That's something you could do about it, Kell. The Texans are scared now, and they've quit driving their stock north. One man could change all that. One man who could ride the border gangs into the dirt and deliver a full-sized herd to Kansas City."

"You asking me to do a thing like that so you can get richer, Mr. McKittridge?"

The railroad man rocked on his heels. His voice was a bellow still, but a muted bellow, thick with emotion. "You misjudge me, Kell. It's not for me that I'm asking anything. I'm asking it for you—for my niece."

He paced across the room, the bones of his big body sagging with defeat. He shook his heavy head. "You think little, Kell, and that worries me. A big man thinks big. You can do big things. Your accomplishments can swallow up the little wrongs you've done. When the world points to you as a man, and people shake your hand for helping the human race, the wrongs will grow smaller. Then you can live with yourself, Kell."

Finished, McKittridge sank into a chair, fishing in his pocket for a cigar. Bennett Kell stared at the space the big man had filled in the room. He stared with eyes that could look backward into a hate-filled past. A few rash acts, spurred by temper and revenge, had trapped him in a life that tortured his conscience.

Now McKittridge had shown him a way out. But it was a rough trail to ride, a trail that would set him against the men who had ridden at his side for nearly a year. Bennett felt no regret at such a prospect, for the bond among such men was one of strength and force

25

and not of friendship. He had found something better here in this room—if he could hold on to it. But now Ada McKittridge knew him for what he was. Would she ever trust her happiness to him?

She was still at his side. He turned his eyes to her, a question in his glance, and Ada was ready with an answer. She said, "You don't have to do a thing to make me love you, Bennett. We can leave Kansas City and no one will ever know about you or me. You don't have to whip the world for me, Bennett."

McKittridge was watching them, cigar poised, bright blue eyes mirroring uneasiness. Bennett met the man's glance, and understanding passed between them. They each needed something from the other, and only through the exchange could one ever look the other in the eye again.

Puffing slowly on the cigar, McKittridge watched and waited. Bennett patted Ada's hand, feeling the warmth of it through his shirt.

"I'll bring you a herd, Mr. McKittridge."

The railroad man nodded. A smile softened his lips. "Among other things, I've been referred to as a king-maker, Kell. I can do as much for you. Bring that herd to the railroad and you'll be the biggest man in Missouri. It's important—if you make it others will follow."

"I'll just want wages and a wife, Mr. McKittridge." He looked down at Ada. "Wait right here for me. I'll be back."

Her fingers dug into his arm and tears sparkled in her eyes. Bennett slipped his arm across her shoulder and she came suddenly close to him, her arms hugging his waist. She raised her lips to meet his, tightening the

26

pressure of her arms, and Bennett could feel the contours of her body molded against his. He kissed her with a fierce hunger, and the warm pressure of her body fired him with desire.

He drew away from her at last, his pulse pounding. He said again, "I'll be back, Ada," and started toward the door, eager to begin his mission. McKittridge, who **had** tactfully turned his back a few minutes earlier, twisted in his chair for a parting wave and Bennett acknowledged the gesture with a nod.

They were waiting for him in the alley. Bennett had left his horse ground-tied, expecting to be gone only a few minutes. Now Toby Rusk stood beside the dun, the reins looped carelessly around his wrist. A few feet away Wally Bryan lounged casually against a stack of empty packing crates.

"Evenin'," Toby Rusk grunted.

Bennett stopped midway between the two, his glance flicking from one to the other. "You know how I feel about people meddling in my affairs, Toby."

Toby Rusk shrugged. "It ain't exactly meddling, Bennett. Me and Wally have been making this trip for some time now, and our curiosity has plumb popped the cap. We don't like no secret deals or nothing like that."

A muscle leaped in Bennett's cheek and his hand settled on the bone handle of his Colt. Even in the darkness he could see Wally Bryan go rigid, and he let his hand slide on down the seam of his pants. Wally Bryan was too handy with a gun and, like Rusk, eager to use it.

Wally's soft voice purred at him from the darkness. "You wouldn't be holding out some sort of kickback on us, would you Bennett?"

"There's a girl up there," Bennett said, not trying to hide the anger in his voice. "She's McKittridge's niece and I figure to marry her some day. It's none of your business, but that's what brought me here."

Toby Rusk grinned, and the vulgarity of the man made Bennett want to spit. Rusk was a rough-looking, barrel-chested man with a cleft chin and thick, moist lips. He had come out of the northwest to ride with the guerrillas during the war, and he'd brought with him the crude manners and coarse talk of the fur trappers. Somewhere along the way a bullet had been fired through Rusk's mouth, passing from cheek to cheek. To the casual observer, the puckered scars looked like dimples, giving Rusk an odd cherubic expression.

"It's been a long time since I've enjoyed the company of a pretty woman," Wally Bryan said musingly. "Sorry, Bennett. I guess it was meddling."

Apologies and oily words came easily to Wally Bryan. He'd practiced them on the river boats while he cheated and stole at cards from St. Louis to New Orleans before the war stopped the traffic. He would be back there now, Bennett thought ruefully, if he hadn't lost his teeth. Wally Bryan still had his dark, wiry handsomeness until he smiled. Then he looked like a grotesque caricature. The butt of a Rebel rifle had knocked his teeth out, but it was the last time a man with a gun in his hand had been that close to Wally Bryan and lived. The nickel-plated Colt on Wally's bony thigh had a hair-trigger, and the skinny hand which reached often for it did so with the speed of lightning.

As Wally Bryan started to turn away, Bennett called out to him with sudden inspiration. "Just so there'll be no doubts—" he said. He unbuttoned his shirt and withdrew his money belt. He tossed it on the ground at Toby Rusk's feet. "You and Wally can take that back and divide it with the rest of the boys. That's my share from the last sale, maybe eighty-ninety dollars."

Rusk pushed at his battered Stetson, frowning incredulously. "That looks like you got suddenly rich, Bennett."

"It means we're breaking up, Toby. I'm through with the whole business. My bedroll hasn't got a thing in it but a ragged blanket and a worn-out pair of levis. You can have that, too."

Coming closer, Wally Bryan gave Bennett a suspicious look from small, china-blue eyes. "You've landed something better?"

Bennett shook his head, moved toward his horse. He took the reins from Toby Rusk and swung up. Then he paused, pressed by the same impulse which had caused him to discard the money belt.

"I figure I better tell you this. I'm heading for Texas to bring back a herd. I don't know whose it will be or when we'll get here, but I aim to deliver it at the railhead. So cut up the gang and scatter out. I'd hate to meet any of you on the way in."

Toby Rusk laughed. "Hell, Bennett, you joshin' us? That's a natural deal. We could throw down on you and you could fake a good fight. But we'd get the cattle. After we sold them you'd get your share, and we could all quit with our pockets full."

"Nothing doing."

Bennett lifted the dun's reins and shoved it around with his knee. He wanted to leave quickly now before

29

he had time to consider Rusk's proposition. To support Ada right, a man would need money. If he let himself discuss the idea with Rusk he would have to fight temptation all the way to Texas. He pushed the thought hastily from his mind and nudged the dun again. But Toby Rusk moved as the horse started forward. He grabbed Bennett's arm and yanked him from the saddle.

It caught Bennett off guard. He landed on his shoulder and rolled, springing up in a half-crouch.

"I hate a yaller-belly," Toby Rusk growled, and stepped in swinging.

A sledging blow peeled skin from Bennett's cheek and brought burning tears to his left eye. He took a part of Rusk's weight against his shoulder, getting inside the man's flailing arms. His first blow came up from his belt, his knotted fist jolting against Rusk's chin. Before Rusk could duck and wheel, Bennett's other fist had cracked against the man's temple, rocking his head.

Rusk backed up a step and Bennett pursued him, ramming an elbow against the man's thick middle, drawing his hands down. With seeming unconcern, Bennett followed the man back a step at a time, raining blows at him. Blood streamed from Rusk's nose, and his breath was coming in snorting gasps. He was too busy retreating to organize a defense, and for a moment Bennett thought the fight was won.

As Rusk crumpled to the ground Bennett stepped in with a sense of triumph. But Rusk had fallen deliberately. His arms shot out, grabbing Bennett's legs. At the same time Rusk jackknifed erect, driving his head into Bennett's mid-section, throwing him to the ground with a jolt that left his senses reeling.

Wally Bryan was ready. His boot lashed out, striking Bennett's temple with a thundering shock. His vision clouded and dizziness gripped him. He reeled half-erect, swinging wildly at the faint image of Toby Rusk's dimpled face.

Rusk ducked the blow and sent a fist into Bennett's stomach. The breath hissed out of him, and he toppled over on his back. Rusk stood astraddle of him, reached down and pulled him up by the shirt front.

"I couldn't let you leave without somethin' to remember us by, Bennett," Rusk said thickly. "This makes it a clean break. You couldn't have a place in our outfit now if you wanted it. But the gang ain't splittin' up. I'm takin' over, that's all. Go on to Texas, Bennett, but you'd best stay there. A man that will pull out on his pards and then turn his gun against them deserves to be shot on sight. Don't come back."

Rusk shoved him back to the ground and stalked away. Wally Bryan went with him, backing stealthily, a gun clenched in his hand.

When the two were gone, Bennett struggled to his feet and staggered to his horse. He rested a moment and then looked around until he found the gun which had fallen from his holster. He shoved it in place. Next time, he'd reach for it sooner.

He mounted and rode south. It was not to his liking to be beaten and run, but he did not feel pressed to seek immediate satisfaction.

He was coming back. He would meet Toby Rusk and Wally Bryan again.

Three

Under the dying rays of the brassy midsummer sun, the waters of the Trinity River shone blood-red. A vagrant breeze stroked the tips of purpling sage and brought a sighing sound from the cottonwoods that hugged the river's edge. In twos and threes, long-horned cattle drifted across the rolling plain to wet their muzzles, then stand with heads swinging and horns clacking in mock combat.

Bennett Kell looked down on them from a slight rise where he had stopped to rest his horse. For the past five days, ever since he'd crossed the Red and touched Texas soil again, he had been in a somber mood. He had counted thousands of cattle and had stopped at a dozen spreads, finding at each the same disquieting scene: a harassed, dispirited rancher in rags and tatters, standing a lone vigil over crumbling hopes.

They were hungry for talk, for friendship, and they welcomed the company of the sun-darkened stranger who came their way on a winded dun horse. They fed him dried beef and coffee brewed from parched barley, but when he talked of a trail drive to Missouri they shook their heads and laughed bitterly.

They had no crew and no money to hire one, and they had heard of the border gangs. They had their cattle and their lives, and they had heard of men who had lost both on their way to Missouri. And then Bennett had heard about a strange man named Ira Borden who ranched on the Trinity and had a cache of gold to hold his crew and the grit of the devil to take him to Missouri. So he had ridden to the Trinity.

He had followed the stream southward with hope building in him, but now he began to feel doubtful about the prospects here. He hooked a leg around the saddle horn, shifting his weight with the studied manner of a man whose strength is waning and who needs to practice economy in every move. The long weeks on the trail had thinned his face and sapped his strength, and the struggle of his own thoughts had frayed his nerves.

This was Texas; this was home, and the sights and smells of it stirred old memories within him and drew him to it. He wanted to ride past here, on to the Brazos and his own ranch. There, as here, were cattle roaming free and unattended. They were his cattle, and they were worth good money in Missouri; worth enough money to give him the start he needed with Ada McKittridge. But what were they saying of him now on the Brazos?

Bennett Kell could guess. He had once turned Yankee, but now he had turned cattle thief. He couldn't go back to the Brazos. Not yet.

His eyes thoughtful, he lifted his gaze from the river to the ramshackle cabin he had spotted when he rode up. It was a drab-looking place, sitting back a hundred yards from a sharp bend of the river. A single horse roamed doggedly around the sagging corral, and a ribbon of smoke drifted lazily from a stovepipe jutting through the roof of the cabin.

Shrugging, Bennett fitted his foot back to the stirrup and kneed the tired dun toward the house.

He rode into the yard, yelling, "Hello, the house!" and then drew rein and waited.

A stocky, gray-eyed man in patched levis and a hide vest stepped from the back door. Bennett guessed his age at fifty, judging by the deep creases around his mouth and the snow in his hair, but he knew it could have been less. A man aged fast under the stresses of the Sixties, and Bennett had the weary feeling that a century had passed since he took to the trail.

The man had a cedar-handled Colt strapped to his leg, and he stopped with his hand resting on it. He said, "I reckon you wouldn't be looking for work where the pay is two meals of beef a day and a promise of good days to come. But if that be it, you've found it."

Bennett shook his head. "Looking for a man who's driving to Missouri. I hear his name is Ira Borden."

"You hear right. But maybe you didn't hear Borden's a damn fool. He'll never make it."

"He'll make it," Bennett said. Long silences had made his voice dry, but excitement was racing through him. "He'll make it if I can find him."

The gray-eyed man cocked his head speculatively. "Want to light for a spell, mister? I could tell you some

34

things. My name's Nat Rickard. I was up the trail in April."

A fiery light leaped in the rancher's eyes, and his lips flattened against his teeth. Somewhere in his mind a memory came alive and filled his face with bitterness. His hand tightened on the gun as he eyed Bennett's face, waiting for a reply.

"I'm in something of a hurry," Bennett said quickly. The man expected him to give his name, but on a hunch Bennett withheld it. "If you could give me some notion of the trail, I'd like to hit Borden's camp before dark."

Rickard waved his hand indifferently. "That'd be a mite of a chore. Borden's got a herd bedded twelve-fifteen miles south, near the river. You could maybe raise him by midnight if that dun could stand up, but it won't."

"I'll try," Bennett said, lifting the reins. "I'm obliged to you, Rickard."

Anger touched Rickard's face again, and Bennett hesitated. "Nobody but fools will go up that trail," Rickard said. "I went. Pulled out of here with eight hundred head, traded a few to the Choctaws and Osages for safe passage, and headed into Missouri with better'n seven hundred. Then the thievin' bastards hit me in the night, killed three of my drovers and sent most of the others high-tailin' it home. But I saved some; maybe two hundred head. I almost made it to the railroad. Then that crazy Texan hit me. Stampeded my cows and took the rest. That's what you'll find on the border, mister. Ira Borden's goin' to get a lot of good men killed, that's all."

Bennett swung the horse around without speaking.

He touched his dusty black hat in salute, and left the bitter, beaten man standing alone in the yellow twilight. As he rode, his hand fell subconsciously to the spot his money belt had formerly occupied around his waist. It would have been better to have kept it, he reflected, and given its contents to Nat Rickard. He didn't remember the man, but he had no doubt about the identity of the "crazy Texan" Rickard had mentioned.

As soon as he was out of sight, he slowed the dun to a moderate canter; the horse wouldn't last much longer without rest. He followed the river for a few miles, stopping at last in a low hollow where the blue-stem brushed at his stirrups. After setting up a picket line so the horse could rest and feed, Bennett propped his head on his saddle and closed his eyes.

But sleep would not come. Weariness was a dull ache through his body, but a driving urgency made him restless. He was too near the end of one trail and the beginning of another and he wanted to consider the things which had brought him here.

Along the trail he had thought only of the vast distances and the searing days and lonely nights which had merged one into the other until he had lost count of time. He had accepted only one delay, that in a motley little town called Outpost. There a horse trader had offered him three dollars to saddle-break a pair of wild remounts scheduled for delivery at an army post farther east. Two of the three dollars had gone for beans and dried beef to tide him over between ranches, but Bennett had squandered the third. He had spent it for cigars, buying six slim panatelas like the ones he'd

36

smoked in McKittridge's hotel suite.

The cigars were a symbol, a tangible link between him and the life he wanted to become a part of. He needed those cigars to keep the dream alive. Out of the swirls of smoke and pungent aroma came visions of the rich tapestry of the Pioneer House and the golden beauty of Ada McKittridge.

Bennett wanted to think of these things, but he was miserly with the cigars. Five of them were still in his saddlebag, wrapped in a neck scarf, and the stub of one was in his shirt pocket. He fished for the stub now, scratching a match aflame with his thumb. His black eyes were squinted as he let the smoke out slowly, his thoughts shifting between Ada McKittridge's last kiss and his meeting with Nat Rickard.

To prove himself worthy of Ada, Bennett had to deliver a herd to the railhead in Missouri. But between the Trinity and Kansas City waited the border gangs, filled with greed and grudges and an abiding hope that a herd such as Ira Borden's would pass their way.

Nat Rickard had been there, and he had warned that Borden's venture would only get some good men killed. No man was more certain of this danger than Bennett Kell.

But if Ira Borden was driving to Missouri, Bennett Kell would go with him. For the love of a girl and the respect of her guardian, he'd fight by Borden's side until they drove the cattle into the loading pens or left their blood on the dark ridges of Missouri.

He picked the fire from the cigar and returned the stub to his pocket. Then he stretched on the ground with his head on the saddle again, a warm contentment relaxing him. He could sleep now, but at daybreak he meant to be talking to Ira Borden. He wished he knew more of the man, especially about the rumor of his gold cache and the motives which spurred him to a task no other would undertake. But there would be time to learn about these things.

It was a long way to Missouri.

Four

A murky mist rose from the river and drifted across the flatlands, almost obscuring the bedding ground of the Horseshoe herd. The mist was like a shroud, gray and flimsy, and perhaps Ira Borden saw in the dreary dawn an ill omen; for he disengaged himself from the deep shadows of the chuck wagon for the first time during his night-long vigil and trudged off toward the herd.

He was a solid black shadow in the mist. He was a big man, Ira Borden; a heavy-bodied, bull-necked, bull-voiced man. He had the hard stride and determined gait of a bull buffalo, and he would walk over the man who failed to move aside to let him pass. At sixty-five, Ira Borden was this kind of man and he let no one forget it.

His high-heeled boot crunched dirt a foot from a blanketed form, and the man within did not move until Borden was ten yards away. Then the man sat erect and called to another nearby. The two of them hunched across the intervening space. They shook their heads in unison.

"Zumbro's going to get spit on," one of them said in a guarded tone.

"If he shows."

"He'll show, and there'll be hell to pay. Borden's been up since midnight. That was the deadline for Zumbro to get back to camp. I'm surprised a man who knows Borden like Wade Zumbro does would run the risk just to tell a chippie good-by."

"Just because Bonnie Gray sings in her old man's saloon doesn't make her a chippie, cowboy. I'd call her a whole heap of woman and not worry much about what kind. I'd have done just what Zumbro did, but I wouldn't let him spit on me."

"As long as Ira Borden holds onto that gold you'd let him."

The sound of a heavy footfall caused them to break apart. They huddled in their blankets again, listening, feigning sleep.

It was Cass Neely, the cook, moving around. Cass threw wood on smoldering embers and rattled it into a blaze. He began clawing provisions from a wagon bed, aware that he'd overslept and worrying about it.

A red glow burned on the eastern horizon, and the mist began to thin. The snap of a blanket being tossed aside was loud in the stillness. Everything was a muted sound thereafter, as the camp wakened to the feel that something was wrong.

Cass Neely muttered under his breath. "Ira must be dead. I never knowed the Horseshoe to start a day's work after daybreak, and I been around these parts nigh twenty years. Wasn't for Clay Macklin and Monte

Cole mumbling in their blankets out there, I might've slept till doomsday."

"Where's Zumbro?" Bert Roscoe asked sleepily. "This is the first mornin' I recollect he ain't kicked me in the belly before the owls stopped hootin'."

"He ain't back from town," Clay Macklin said.

"Good," Roscoe grunted. "I hope Borden stomps his guts out. Borden said nobody could leave camp the last night before we hit the trail. Then he lets Zumbro sneak out provided he reports in at midnight. Zumbro may be the ramrod here, but other men besides him can find a girl to—"

Ira Borden, coming up on the blind side of the chuck wagon, stepped into view and Bert Roscoe's harangue ended in a hacking cough. Borden leaned his elbows on a wagon rim and let his flat stare settle on Roscoe for a moment. Roscoe met his glance, leaning forward slightly to do it, as though the force of Borden's frosty eyes would topple him backward unless he did.

"We sit another day," Borden said. "Macklin, you and Roscoe wolf your grub and go send the nighthawks in. The rest of you oil your harness and clean your guns. Both will likely be in for a lot of wear."

Ira Borden turned his back on them and stared south, toward town. It didn't matter to him that they resented the orders. A man's system gets keyed up for a trail drive. He gets ready for restless sun, driving rain, eternal movement and eternal dust. He's a spring wound tight, and straining for release. And, like a spring, his strength ebbs when the release is delayed. The Horseshoe crew knew this, and they cringed at the prospect of idleness.

Zumbro rode in as the first men to finish eating were

41

rinsing tin plates in the water barrel beside the chuck wagon. He was not alone. Bonnie Gray came with him, riding a prancing pinto and carrying a bulky blanket roll and a cracked valise behind the saddle.

Ira Borden stared at them. His shaggy gray hair, riding close to his threadbare collar, bristled like porcupine quills. His frost-gray eyes froze in his face, and a pulse throbbed at his temple. But his voice was muted, coming as a hoarse rumble in his chest. He said, "Step down, Zumbro."

Wade Zumbro shifted in his saddle. He was cut from the same mold as Borden, but on a lesser scale. He was a stocky, slope-shouldered man of twenty-five with the glittering wildness of youth in his blue eyes and the wisdom of age in the moody caution with which he tackled problems. His dress was the faded and patched remnants of a Confederate uniform, but it had a scrubbed-clean freshness about it. Zumbro had found his passion for cleanliness appealed to women, and he practiced it diligently.

He sat in his saddle. Mounted he could look down at Ira Borden; afoot he would have to look up. And Wade Zumbro was a man who would think about this and its effect on others. He said, "Two minutes, Ira. I'll talk two minutes and then I'll step down."

The crew was watching. Ranged around Ira Borden were ten men who moved when he walked; ten men who'd never seen an order questioned or a command disobeyed. They waited, pretending to be busy with blankets and gear, and a green twig simmered plaintively on the cook fire.

"You'll step down or ride out." Borden's voice rose to its full volume now, echoing hollowly in the mist-laden air. Borden's knobby right hand moved to the cedar butt of his gun. It was a big gun, a .44 Colt, riding snugly in a cutaway holster on his right leg.

Zumbro matched the move. Not as boldly did his hand move, but his palm opened on the pommel and his elbow crooked so he could get to his own .45 in a hurry. Zumbro said, "I'll ride out for back wages, Ira, or I'll ride to Missouri for wages and the extra ante you promised."

Every word was measured. There was no mockery, no badgering in Zumbro's tone. He'd thought about it on the way in, and he'd said the right thing. Borden had the money, had it in gold coin, which, perhaps, was the greatest oddity known in this barren, poverty-pinched year after the war. While he held the money he held his crew. Without it he would be just another helpless Texan, surrounded by cattle and despair, unable to reach the only market which promised hard cash for beef. He couldn't pay Zumbro now. When he opened his cache, the wolves would be on him. Ten men would demand their money, take it once the move was made, and then the men would ride away to leave him with an empty pocket and a herd that was worthless where it stood. Zumbro had thought it out, and now he sat his saddle and waited.

"Take your two minutes," said Borden. He took a heavy brass watch from his pocket. His frost-gray eyes left Zumbro's face and fastened on the watch, and there was no indication that he listened to his foreman's words.

Zumbro looked across at Bonnie Gray for the first time since they had arrived. She was an olive-skinned girl of twenty with the delicate facial structure and ripe, pouting mouth so usual in those of mixed blood lines. There was a cold calm in the way she sat her horse, her chin lifted haughtily while she waited for the incident to run its course. Zumbro looked at her ebony black hair glistening in the rising sun, looked at her flaring hips and swelling breasts, and then into her moody brown eyes. He winked and turned back toward Borden.

"She goes with me, Ira. This is a one-way ride. We all know that. So Bonnie and me aim to be married in Missouri and stay up in that country. That's why I brought her, Ira. I'd never see her again if I hadn't. The carpetbaggers and land crooks are out to bust Texas, Ira, and there's nothing here for us. She can stand the ride; she can even help Cass some. She——"

Ira Borden stuffed the brass watch back into his shirt pocket. "Time's up. Step down, Zumbro."

"You ain't arguing the point, Ira?"

"I ain't arguing. Step down, Zumbro."

Bonnie Gray cried. "Wait, Wade. Let's——"

But Zumbro did not wait. He swung lightly to the ground. His hatbrim was on a level with Borden's eyes, and they were two feet apart. Ira Borden cleared his throat and spat.

Zumbro jumped backward, bumping his horse. He cursed in a choked, startled wheeze. He looked down at the spittle clinging to the front of his clean shirt, and then back at Ira Borden. But Borden's back was turned toward him. The foreman's clenched fists relaxed. His shoulders slumped and he raised sheepish eyes to look at the crew. No one looked at him.

They had seen it, but they had not wanted to see it. Until now, they had not believed the things they'd heard of Ira Borden. But they'd been afraid of this. It

44

had started in his young days, and not a man of this crew had been on the Horseshoe then. But the story had been told in cow-camps from the Rio to the Mogollons, from the Mississippi to the Sierras: Ira Borden never fired a man; he just spat on him and the man could quit or turn to dirt. The filth of it was worse than a curse, the sting to a man's pride worse than a lashing.

Ten seconds passed. Wade Zumbro's breath hissed and subsided in his throat, and at last he ripped off his neckerchief and scrubbed it across his shirt front. When he had finished, he threw the scarf to the earth and ground it under his heel. He started toward Bonnie Gray's horse, but Borden's voice stopped him in his tracks.

Borden was barking orders. "Monte . . . Scrap! The two of you nail Zumbro and hold him. Do it now. From this time on, ten dollars comes off that hundred-dollar bonus every time a man disobeys an order."

Scrap Dooley and Monte Cole strode toward Zumbro. The foreman spread his feet and hunched his shoulders. He welcomed a fight. He wanted to hit something or somebody, even an old man like Monte Cole and a beanpole like Scrap Dooley who were only obeying orders. But he forgot to think about Ira Borden.

Scrap and Monte were only to distract him. A lass rope whistled in the air and a loop settled around Zumbro's shoulders. An expert flip sent the rope sliding over his arms; a swift yank drew it tight. Zumbro stood helpless, staring over Monte Cole's shoulder as Ira Borden tightened the slack on the rope and walked toward him.

"You're making a bad enemy, Ira," Zumbro said quietly. "You need me. I gave you my word I'd drive this herd to Missouri and I'll keep it. To get there I'll hold this crew together, and that's something you can't do, Ira. Even if you're holding up their pay they'll quit you unless there's somebody to hold them together. They'll figure six months' work is easier to lose than a life. My word stands if you'll let Bonnie come along."

Zumbro's lips thinned and his voice softened. "I remember the vaquero you tied up to a wagon wheel all day because he broke a bronc's wind, Ira. You'll be sorry if you do that to me."

Borden stopped. His wide lips hardened and his frost-gray eyes flicked from Zumbro to the girl and back again. He slacked off on the rope, then tossed the end into the dirt.

"I've lost a day I can't get back, Zumbro. I'll call it settled. But there's one responsibility I don't take. One woman and ten men who haven't had the money to visit a bistro in five years won't mix. Don't holler for me when somebody takes her for the night."

Zumbro took the time to hunt out each man with his eyes and look him in the face. "When that happens, Ira, you'll have a funeral on your hands."

Again Zumbro found himself staring at the rancher's wide back. Borden was moving toward the fire. Cass Neely, fidgeting and uneasy, had kept the food warm. He handed Borden a heaping plate, then stepped back as though standing sentry duty.

Neely was ferret-eyed and nervous and his gaze was forever roving from place to place. So it was he who first saw the rider approaching the Horseshoe camp.

46

The rider came up from the river, his clothing soggy and his line-backed dun flinching and slobbering to rid itself of water. Cass nudged Ira Borden's shoulder, and the rancher looked up. A frown drew Borden's shaggy white brows close to his eyes and he put down his plate and stood up.

Borden continued to study the horseman, cataloguing the weariness in the sun-blistered face, the firm seat in the saddle, the handy slant of the bone-handled Colt which had been fastened to the saddle horn for the river crossing.

Borden did not move until the river had stopped his horse. There was blunt curiosity in the rancher's eyes, a patient curiosity.

"Morning," the rider said. "If you're Ira Borden my name's Bennett Kell. If you're not I'm just a no-good cuss looking for the end of the rainbow."

"I'm Borden."

Bennett nodded, smiled with relief. "Could we talk somewhere?"

"Anything you have to say can be said here. What's on your mind?"

"I hear you're driving north. I want a job—a special job. I want to hire on as your ramrod."

A step behind Ira Borden, a handsome, dark-haired puncher sprang to his feet. He said, "We got a ramrod, mister. Me—Wade Zumbro."

Borden did not look around. He kept his eyes on Bennett Kell, his seamed face expressionless. "One man stands about the same chance as another against

47

the border gangs, Kell. What makes you think you can ride in here and make yourself top dog at the bat of an eye?"

Bennett sat his horse and looked about him. Borden's men were watching him guardedly. He had noticed the girl earlier, but now his eyes lingered on her face. She was smiling at him, as though amused by the tension his arrival here had created. Bennett let the silence drag on for seconds.

"I'm the only man in Texas who can guarantee you safe passage to Missouri," he said at length. "I can deliver your herd to the Kansas City railhead. I swear it."

The certainty Ira Borden saw in the lean, intent face impressed him. He looked at Bennett with interest in the frost-gray eyes. "What makes you something special?" he asked.

Bennett had known from the beginning that the question would come, and there was only one answer that could be convincing. He said, "I know where the border gangs are and how to get by them. They'll let me through—because I've been running a gang myself."

He was watching Ira Borden and almost missed Wade Zumbro's move. But Zumbro had to sidestep to get from behind Borden, and Bennett saw a flash of sunlight as the Horseshoe foreman brought his gun up.

Five

Wade Zumbro's weapon was already clear of leather and lifting into line for a shot. Bennett swiveled a shoulder to get at the Colt tied to his saddle. He braced for Zumbro's shot, knowing he would never match it. But the shot never came. Through a haze of icy fear he saw the calm shift of Ira Borden's body. A quick move, a low curse from Wade Zumbro, a sharp command from the side of the big rancher's mouth.

These things Bennett was aware of in the fleeting seconds, and Ira Borden was standing directly in front of Wade Zumbro again. The foreman could not shoot without firing through the rancher's body.

"I said put it away, Zumbro." Borden's voice lashed at the foreman. And Borden stood his ground until he heard the hiss of gun metal sliding against leather.

Borden's frosty eyes lifted to Bennett's tense face, and a dry chuckle rattled his throat. "I've just saved your life, Kell. Now I feel I can trust you. You owe me something. Rest your horse and have a bite to eat. I've had some trouble with one of my men, and I'm glad to make a change. You're the ramrod, Kell, starting now. Later I'll want to talk."

Turning on his heel, Borden stalked off toward the rope corral where the wrangler was holding his horse. Wade Zumbro was left staring into Bennett Kell's face. White lines stretched away from Zumbro's hard-drawn lips and his eyes were afire with fury. His right arm was still crooked away from his holstered gun and his knees were bent in a springy crouch.

Bennett swung to the ground, deliberately turning his back on Zumbro. He grasped the dun's reins and led him off toward the remuda himself, feeling the tension of the camp behind him. There had been trouble here before he came and it was not yet over. From the brush along the creek he had seen Zumbro ride in with the girl, and had watched the by-play that resulted. He could only guess at the reasons behind the argument between Borden and Wade Zumbro, but of one thing he was sure: A trail drive was no place for a woman.

Especially a woman with the sensuous mouth and hungry eyes of that one.

The boss wrangler was a wizened, tobacco-chewing man named Ben Lufton. He had been briefed by Ira Borden a moment before, and he met Bennett with a measured, quizzical glance. He took the dun's reins, clucked his tongue at the horse's gaunted flanks, then chuckled approvingly as Bennett removed the saddle and checked carefully for raw spots beneath the blanket.

"Always glad to see any man who rides a double-cinched rig," Ben Lufton drawled at last. "That's Texas in any language."

Bennett shouldered the saddle and grunted under its

50

weight. "You can buy a saddle like this in Montana or Arkansas," he murmured, and seeing Lufton's scowl added, "but I didn't. Bought it at Gray's Saddlery on the Brazos."

He started off toward the camp, slowing his pace when he found Lufton still at his side. The wrangler cleared his throat experimentally, then said, "When you fight Wade Zumbro don't expect it to be fair."

"You think we'll fight?"

"Know you will. Before the day's out. It has to come and Borden will welcome it. The boys are edgy because they didn't get started up the trail. It'll take their minds off their own aggravation and have 'em in better spirits for tomorrow. But don't expect it to be fair. Wade Zumbro washes clean but he fights dirty."

"I'll remember. Thanks."

Cass Neely had the coffee pot filled and a plate of beef and beans warming near the fire when Bennett tossed his saddle down and sat on it. Cass started to get the food when he saw Bennett, but the girl reached the fire first. She had been sitting in the sparse shade of a manzanita bush watching Bennett through half-shut eyes. She moved with a quick deerlike grace and she was standing beside Bennett almost as soon as he was seated.

"I'm Bonnie Gray," she said, handing him the plate. "I know who you are, of course. You are a thief."

The drovers lounging around the camp swung their eyes toward Bennett and he felt anger tearing through him. He sprang to his feet, grabbing at the girl's arm as she started away from him.

She came easily—too easily. As he swung her around she allowed the momentum to carry her against him.

51

The firm pressure of her breasts was against his arm, and her breath, coming from slightly parted lips, was hot against his throat as she looked defiantly up into his face.

Then she laughed—a teasing, provocative laugh. She surrendered to his grasp, her brown eyes daring him. And in her whole manner was the unspoken question: "What next?"

Realizing the helplessness of his position, Bennett shoved her roughly away from him. Through clenched teeth he said, "I'm ashamed of what I was. You keep playing games like you just did and you'll be sorry for what you are. The only thing you'll need to know about me is that I'm bossing this drive. You'll stay with it only as long as I want you to. Think about that."

A shiny light burned in Bonnie Gray's eyes and her full mouth pouted at him. She started to say something but changed her mind. She shrugged and turned away, going toward the pinto which stood nearby. Bennett wanted to ignore her, but he found himself watching the rhythm of her hips and the way the soft folds of the divided skirt clung to her round thighs. She mounted the horse and rode off slowly toward the river.

At Bennett's elbow Cass Neely said, "Wade Zumbro's over that way. She's the girl he's taking to Missouri to marry. When she tells him you gave her a push there's going to be trouble."

Bennett smiled wryly. "The trouble was already made."

He settled himself on the saddle again and picked at the food, his appetite dulled by bad temper. The cook came to sit beside him, bringing the coffee pot, and Bennett began to get acquainted with the Horseshoe crew.

They sat in a scattered circle, playing match poker, fiddling with gear or just staring into space. As Cass Neely introduced them they gave bare signs of recognition. Some nodded dourly, some tipped hatbrims with a forefinger, some merely lifted their glance to study Bennett Kell's dark face.

This was the way it went when there was a change in authority among men such as these. Among them all there was not a weak will or a soft hand. They had been baked hard by the merciless sun, toughened by the obstacles this raw land threw against every man who took his living from it. Their loyalty went only to a man who was stronger or whose skill was a shade above their own. They knew Zumbro, but Kell was a stranger. They were waiting for him to prove he was a better man than Zumbro.

And at the end of a long trail Big Jim McKittridge waited, too. McKittridge waited for a herd that would bring support for his railroad and an accomplishment that would prove Bennett Kell was too big to let a few misdeeds brand him for life.

Sweat stood on Bennett's brow as the blazing Texas sun climbed into the sky and curled the sage with its heat. But a cold chill rode along his spine and knotted his stomach. There was going to be trouble from this day on, and Borden's gold and Zumbro's girl would be a constant temptation to the Horseshoe crew.

Bennett Kell told himself that neither would tempt him. No, neither one. No, by God . . .

By the time he had finished eating, the taut atmosphere of the camp was beginning to wear on his nerves. He rinsed his tin plate in the water barrel beside the chuck wagon and took the cigar stub from his shirt pocket. The aroma of the smoke brought quick glances from the others and Bennett was aware that he must present a peculiar sight.

"A habit I picked up in K.C.," he explained, then turned away as he saw that the Horseshoe crew interpreted the gesture as a display of superiority.

He walked off toward the river. He had shaved and bathed at his night camp but his worn moleskins were stiff with dust and sweat and he thought he would take a swim while he washed them. Before he had gone twenty yards he changed his mind. Wade Zumbro was sulking among the willows along the river and he was in a murderous mood. Perhaps a fight between them was inevitable but Bennett didn't want to hasten it.

As he started to turn back, Bert Roscoe rode toward him from the grazing grounds. The horse stopped a few feet away and Roscoe stepped to the ground, sleeving sweat from his freckled face. He was a loose-jointed, angular man with fiery red hair and deep laugh lines at the corners of his wide mouth.

"The Great Man wants words with you, Kell," Roscoe said. "He's with the herd. Counting his cows to make sure the nighthawks didn't eat none, I reckon."

"You mean Borden?"

"Who else? Here, take my horse. I ain't goin' nowhere. Or maybe I will. Maybe I'll slip into Crosscut and fetch me a gal out here to keep me company on the way to Missouri. Could I bring one for you, Kell?"

Bennett laughed. He said, "Got one in Missouri," and swung aboard Bert Roscoe's roan.

The redhead was still watching him, his head cocked speculatively. "That why you repentin' for your sins, cowboy?"

54

Bennett let the question go unanswered. He didn't want to talk about his association with the border gangs, least of all the resentment he'd stirred in Toby Rusk. There was no way of knowing what lay ahead of them, and he didn't want the Horseshoe thinking they would have to fight his personal battle before they could deliver a herd.

With the drive scheduled at dawn, the Horseshoe herd was being kept in close order on a patch of graze bounded on three sides by a sharp U-turn of the river. Riders patrolled the open end of the U, swinging lariats occasionally to keep the cattle from scattering over the plain. From atop a small hogback which hid the cattle from the campsite, Bennett got his first full view of the herd. For a moment his worries were forgotten. It was good to see cattle bunched again, good to hear the slap of switching trails and the incessant snick-snick of tearing grass. He judged there were better than fifteen hundred head under the Horseshoe brand, and he did some quick figuring. Borden would collect thirty thousand dollars in cash when they reached Kansas City. Bennett could visualize the pleasure such a shipment would bring to Jim McKittridge. But Toby Rusk would look upon the herd with equal joy.

A movement at the fringe of the herd caught his eye, and he saw Ira Borden standing in the shade of a post-oak, waving his hat for attention. When Bennett drew rein beside him, Borden sat down with his back against the tree and said, "Rest yourself, Kell, and we'll have that talk now."

Dismounting, Bennett squatted on his heels beside the man, meeting Borden's frosty gaze and waiting for him to speak. Borden took his time, as though he had forgotten Bennett's presence and become lost in a reverie.

At last he said, "Lots of things could happen in this deal with you, Kell. You could string me along until we reached your gang and then sell me out. You could hang around until you figured out where I carry my gold and then steal it. You could turn my crew against me and steal my herd. I'm sure you've heard I've got some gold, and you admit you've been a thief."

"But you don't think I'll do any of those things, do you?"

"No. I didn't think so from the time you told me you'd run a border gang. Telling me that seemed like it was important to you, like you had to get it off your chest. I saved your life, and you strike me as a man who'd consider that a bond between us. I'll ask you one question. What made you decide to pull out of the gangs up north?"

"A woman," Bennett said. "A good woman—one who won't be saddled with a nothing and a nobody. I want to marry her and bring her to Texas, but I want her to be able to walk down the street with me and hold her head up proud when she does it."

Borden nodded. "It's sent many a man straight, loving a woman has." He paused, adding, "And many a man wrong."

The rancher rose, his eyes turned toward the ground, his brows furrowed. He walked to his horse and stood with an arm resting on the pommel.

"You'll want to keep a close eye on Zumbro. The other men will be all right once we get started. They've been with me six months—all except Cass Bailey. Cass has worked on the Horseshoe for twenty years. So far

56

they've had no pay. That's the only way I'd ever get them to risk a drive to Kansas City. Whether we sell the cattle or not they know I've got the money to pay them and that makes them hang on. I've showed each of them a handful of gold coins and they'll stick until they get it."

He mounted and rode away, expecting no comment and getting none. Bennett was glad to be alone. The fatigue of the trail was still in his bones, and he needed rest and time to think. He propped his back against the post-oak, slanted his hat brim over his eyes and tried to take a nap. Sleep came hard to him because his mind kept reminding him of the real reason for this unaccustomed leisure: He was trying to build his strength for the fight with Wade Zumbro.

About noon he rode the roan in a wide circle around the upper edge of the herd, stopping to pass the time of day with the riders he had not met at the camp. Later he cut back to the river where he soaked the dirt from his clothes, hanging them on cottonwood boughs to dry while he lounged in the tepid water. He returned to the Horseshoe camp just as Cass Neely was dishing up the evening meal.

There was no change in the mood of the place. Men were scattered about in twos and threes, eating silently. Wade Zumbro and Bonnie Gray were sitting close to each other beyond the fire, talking in whispers. As Bennett walked in from the horse corral he saw the girl's glance hover on him a moment before she put her lips close to Zumbro's ear and said something. Zumbro nodded without looking up, and Bennett felt his stomach knot.

Nodding to the group in general, Bennett sought out

Bert Roscoe with his eyes and said, "Left your pony with the wrangler."

"Thought you'd stole him," Roscoe murmured around a mouthful of food. "Glad you didn't."

"Cattle was his game," Wade Zumbro said loudly. "Didn't you hear, Bert?"

Fury flooded through Bennett's veins and he stopped in his tracks, fists clenched. From the side of the chuck wagon, Ira Borden's stern voice broke through the sudden silence.

"That'll do, Zumbro. Fill your plate, Kell, and sit here with me."

The crew relaxed. Even Wade Zumbro's shoulders seemed to sag slightly, and he shifted around to put his back toward the others. The only defiance came from Bonnie Gray. She laughed—a throaty, mysterious chuckle that could mean anything or nothing. Again her eyes flashed at Bennett. Then she tossed her ebony hair and turned her slim back on the crew, too.

Borden took no notice of Bennett's presence. He finished his meal without speaking again, and smoked a cigarette while Bennett ate. Bennett rose to wash his plate and Borden said, "I'd like to get everything settled before tomorrow, Kell. You and Zumbro can have that fight now."

Borden's voice was loud enough to carry across the camp, and the tone was as impersonal as if he was borrowing a match. Bennett tossed his tin plate into the water and left it there. Turning, he set his hands on his hips and stared at Ira Borden, the heat of anger burning in his eyes.

"You got some rules, too, Borden?"

"Yes, I have. Unbuckle your belt and drop your gun

58

here." He tapped the earth in front of him and looked across at Wade Zumbro. "Come on, Wade. Let's get at it. Tomorrow we drive cows."

Zumbro was already on his feet. A grim smile pulled at his lips, and sweat had put a sheen on his smooth, handsome face. As he strode forward, Bennett's glance went beyond him to Bonnie Gray. She had jumped to her feet with Zumbro, her face flushed with excitement. She stood now with hands braced on her hips, her body swaying with a restless rhythm. A light danced in her eyes, and her red lips were parted. A shiver ran through her, and the reaction gave her away. In the prospect of violence Bonnie Gray found more than excitement, Bennett surmised; she found satisfaction for a deep physical hunger and perhaps this was one explanation of her presence here.

A quick yank and a tug freed Bennett's gunbelt. He dropped it at Borden's feet and stepped aside, waiting for Zumbro. He kept his eyes on the man, measuring his hard, sloping shoulders and bulging arms. In height and reach Bennett had a slight advantage, but their weight was even.

Zumbro was being annoyingly slow and deliberate. His fingers toyed with the belt buckle, letting the notches out one at a time. When the weight of the holstered gun dropped the belt earthward, Zumbro clung to one end of it. The taunting smile was still on his face.

Bennett fidgeted uneasily, trying to watch everything at once. Suddenly Zumbro crouched, his legs widespread. Then he whirled, the gunbelt gripped in both hands. Like a scythe, the belt slashed the air and smacked across Bennett Kell's face.

The first sensation was raw, stinging pain. Bennett felt himself staggering backward, his head roaring with shock. He fell with the taste of blood in his mouth.

Above the clamor of his pulsing blood and the shouts of the crew, two voices clanged like bells in his ears. Ira Borden was bellowing, "Drop it, Zumbro!" and Bonnie Gray was screaming: "Use your spurs on him, Wade!"

Six

Through pain-filled eyes Bennett saw Wade Zumbro coming at him, feet-first. The paling sunlight glinted on big Mexican spurs and Bennett rolled away in desperation.

He didn't quite make it. A knife-slash of pain shot through his left shoulder. Overbalanced by the leap, Zumbro fell heavily beside him. Bennett got his elbows under him and pushed himself to his knees. He rested there, swaying slightly, while he watched Zumbro roll away and bounce to his feet.

The Horseshoe man had the frozen grin on his face again. He charged forward, one fist cocked for a clubbing blow. A senseless, unfeeling fury exploded within Bennett. He bobbed erect, lips drawn back from gritted teeth, his hands locked in front of him, the knuckles of intertwined fingers white with tautness. He stood facing Zumbro, feet braced. As Zumbro came within striking distance, the locked hands lifted like a catapult. Zumbro's swinging arm was knocked aside. Bennett's twin fists caught Zumbro beneath the chin,

61

rocking the man's head back.

A stunned groan passed Zumbro's lips. His feet slipped from under him and he fell on his face, his eyes dilated like those of a man at the end of a hangrope. He lifted a feeble arm as Bennett dived on top of him, fists pumping. Bennett's blows found a mark. He drew blood from Zumbro's nose and raised a lump under one eye. Zumbro fought back, but Bennett kept smashing his fists into the man's face, unmindful of the uneasy silence which had fallen over the camp.

Twisting, flailing and gasping, they rolled and rumbled on the trampled plain. After ten minutes some of the men turned away, sickened by the animal savagery which gripped the two men on the ground.

They rose and fell a dozen times, both oblivious to the world around them, both bloody and winded. The left side of Bennett's face was afire with pain where Zumbro's gunbelt had peeled skin from it. His shirt dangled in tatters across his knotted shoulders, and blood oozed from the ragged gash made by Zumbro's spur.

His vision was foggy, but his muscles were loose and warm. He had no thought of surrendering to the pain, and no tricks which would end the fight quickly. He was conscious only that he was into it, that he had been pushed to violence to satisfy the whim of Ira Borden and the Horseshoe crew. They should have known what kind of man was required to control a border gang. But they wanted proof and he meant to give it to them.

Zumbro tried another lunging charge but Bennett blocked him with his hip. He looped his arm around the man's neck and caught him like a bulldogged steer.

62

With Zumbro's head locked under his armpit, Bennett still had one hand free. He used it like a swinging club, driving the fist methodically into Zumbro's bleeding face.

At last Zumbro's legs went limp. His knees buckled and his falling weight pulled his head free. He fell flat on his face, making retching sounds against the earth.

Bennett stood over him. Blood dripped from his raw knuckles and stained the dust in front of him. He stared at his swollen hands for a moment as though they were not a part of him. Slowly he bent and wrapped his fingers through the thick strands of Zumbro's black hair. Grimacing, he lifted the man a foot off the ground, dropped him, and started to do it again.

A croaking whisper came from Zumbro's split lips. "Let it go, Kell, I'm—whipped."

As the excitement died in him Bennett's legs felt as if they were filled with sand. He wanted to drop to the ground where he was, to lie there until his lungs stopped burning and the red mist evaporated from his eyes. But somehow it seemed important to stay on his feet a while longer, and he turned and walked away.

Like a sleepwalker he strode to the side of the buckboard, stooped and retrieved his gunbelt. Then he eased gently to the ground, his back against the wagon wheel. He tilted his head back, mouth open, and gulped cool, fresh air into his stinging lungs. The broad sky was a deep violet and the northern stars were already flickering alight. It seemed impossible that the gloomy shadows of dusk were creeping along the earth and that the fight had lasted so long.

"You'll need some clothes to ride in tomorrow," Ira Borden said calmly at his side. "I noticed you didn't carry anything in here but saddlebags. There's a harness wagon over beyond the corral. You'll find some extra shirts and levis in it."

Bennett glanced aside at the rancher, somewhat surprised to find him seated just where he had been when the fight began. He said, "Thanks, Borden," feeling that there should be much more to say to this cold-eyed old man who manipulated the lives of others as though they were puppets on a string.

Borden dug a blanket roll from the pile beneath the wagon, rose and walked off to make his bed where the grass was soft and untrampled. A short distance away, he stopped and looked back at the men scattered around the camp. "With one man or ten, I take to the trail tomorrow. If anybody tries to leave camp tonight I'll hear them. I plan to sleep light."

Only Wade Zumbro made a reply. He was sitting erect on the ground with Bonnie Gray kneeling beside him brushing at his battered face with a neck scarf.

Zumbro pushed the girl's arm away and said, "What about me, Ira? Where do I stand?"

"Talk to Kell. He's the ramrod," Borden said, and continued on his way.

Until the question came Bennett had given no thought to Zumbro's future status with the trail crew. The wise thing to do was to fire Zumbro here and now. He would be rid of an enemy and a troublemaker at the same time, for Bonnie Gray would go with Zumbro. But it was a long way to Missouri and every turn of the trail would hold the threat of danger. Zumbro was a capable fighter with his fists or his gun; Bennett was sure of that. . . .

"What about it, Kell?" Zumbro asked flatly.

Bennett looked at the man, finding Zumbro's pale eyes steady and unashamed under his gaze. He said, "Suit yourself, Zumbro. I figure things are settled between us."

"So do I." Zumbro rubbed a sleeve gingerly across his swollen lips and got to his feet. "Think I'll walk over to the river and wash up," he mumbled, and moved off in slow, uncertain steps.

The camp resumed its normal routine. The first pair of nighthawks went out to assume the duties vacated by the day herders and Cass Bailey started stowing his stores for the long drive ahead. Cigarettes began to glow in the gloom and men hunkered around the fire to reminisce a bit. Anticipation and anxiety drove the tension out of the air, and the talk was of river crossings and trail markers and land most of them had never seen.

Bennett kept to himself. His muscles throbbed with weariness, and a multitude of separate pains hammered at his senses. The inside of his mouth was raw and sore and both his eyes were swollen. His head drooped forward on his chest and he sat in a sort of coma, not quite asleep and not quite awake.

Presently he was conscious of something cool and soothing touching the gash on his cheek. He looked up to find Bonnie Gray on her knees beside him. She had a pan of water and was wiping away the crusted blood with a damp cloth. In the starlight her moody eyes were dark pools.

"You looked miserable," she said simply. "I had to do something."

Bennett offered no objections. She leaned close to him, dabbing at his sore cheek, and he studied the

65

supple movement of her shoulders. Her black hair glistened under the starshine, and her full mouth looked soft and moist and appealing. It nettled Bennett that his pulse quickened with her nearness, and at last he caught her hands and pushed them away, not ungratefully.

"You ought to be with Zumbro," he said.

"Wade will be all right as soon as he cleans himself up. This morning a man spit on him and tonight a man whipped him, and all he can think to do is wash his face."

"That shows he's got sense. You talk like you want him to keep after me."

She shook her head. "It's not you Wade hates. The fight with you just gave him an excuse to work off steam. He should go after Borden."

"You sure like a fight, don't you?" Bennett said, a note of scorn in his voice.

Bonnie sat down, doubling her legs beneath her. Her eyes brightened and her chin lifted defiantly. "Why shouldn't I? All my life I've practically lived in my old man's saloon. A fight was the only thing that ever happened to break the monotony. Then it was like the Fourth of July or something. And when it was over I always wanted to kiss the winner. Most women are like that. They always imagine the fight was over them—or they wish it was."

Bonnie's face came close to his, her voice a husky whisper, and Bennett thought she was going to kiss him. He said quickly, "You and Zumbro ought to pull out of this outfit and get married. You should have married him before you came to this camp."

She straightened, her eyes flashing. "You open up

66

Borden's gold cache and pay Wade what's coming to him. That's when we'll get married. Wade won't agree to a wedding until he's got some kind of stake. We'll be married in Missouri. If we get to Missouri."

"We'll get there."

Rising, she held the pan of water in both hands and stared thoughtfully into it. "Maybe," she murmured softly, "Borden doesn't have any gold. I'd like to get one look at it—just to be sure."

Without glancing at him again she disappeared behind the wagon. But he remembered the look on her face and it disturbed him. When Bonnie Gray spoke of Ira Borden's gold a light leaped in her sultry eyes. He'd seen the same look in the eyes of men when they raked in a pot from a poker table.

Overnight the change came. Men woke with smiles on their faces and got up with a spring in their step. Shadows moved with lively purpose through the chill morning darkness as the riders loaded gear and blankets in the harness wagon and selected mounts from the remuda. From the river bank a lilting voice sang snatches of a dance-hall tune.

Bennett sat up and listened. Bonnie Gray sang of a woman with a tainted name, and of a strange, dauntless cowboy who saved her from a life of shame. Her voice carried clearly on the fog-laden air, and there was something of a dreaming schoolgirl in the melancholy tones of it.

A rousing laugh from the direction of the fire drowned out the song, and Bennett turned his attention that way. Bert Roscoe was joshing his sidekick, Monte

Cole, about a widow in Laredo and the whole crew joined in the laughter.

Bennett's spirits lifted. The magic spell of a trail drive was upon the Horseshoe crew, and today their gripes and grudges would be forgotten. The riding, roping, branding and hazing was over; the long days of waiting were at an end. Their thoughts were not of the longer days ahead, the endless miles under blistering sun, stifling dust and driving rains. No man let his mind touch on the countless dangers that could come from a stampeding herd or a border ruffian's rifle. These were men who had come home from war to a broken, poverty-ridden land with no money in their pockets and none to be found. Now there was hope. At the end of the trail their pockets would jingle. They could buy a drink, a new hat, a woman or perhaps make a start of their own.

Someone saw Bennett's silhouette, and a voice from the fire said, "Better grab your cup and claim your turn, Kell. Cass says this is the last of the real coffee. From here on it's grain and branch water!"

"Soon as I can find a shirt and some britches," Bennett said, and rose to seek out the harness wagon. He found clothes to fit and returned a few minutes later, leading his own line-backed dun. Another day's rest would have been good for the animal, but like most men who ever started a trail drive Bennett needed something for luck. So he rode the dun.

Breakfast was finished quickly, hastened by the urging of Cass Bailey, who was packing pots and pans into the wagon as quickly as they were emptied. Bennett looked around for Ira Borden and not finding him asked Wade Zumbro to make the day's riding assignments.

Zumbro looked at him through swollen eyes. His lips were bruised and misshapen but he managed a grateful grin. He knew the men's strength and weaknesses and he knew names Bennett was likely to miss. He reeled them off. Monte Cole, Bert Roscoe, Luke Ashley, Shad Miller on the flanks. Farley Jones and Clay Macklin at swing.

Zumbro paused, said: "That leaves two men. Scrap Dooley and me. There's point and drag spots left. You pick them, Kell."

It was Zumbro's way of finding whether Bennett was still angry and what treatment he could expect in the future. On point, ahead of the herd, went a trail crew's best man; in the drag, one with plodding patience and a willingness to swallow the dust of all who passed first.

Without hesitation Bennett said, "You take point, Zumbro." He glanced beyond the man, nodding at Bonnie Gray, who was standing beside the chuck wagon. "And that leaves her," he said. "I believe she's your responsibility."

Bonnie Gray tossed her hair and smiled. It was as though she had been waiting for this moment. "You can forget me," she said. "Mr. Borden has asked me to ride the harness wagon with him."

Pale spots appeared at the points of Wade Zumbro's ruddy cheeks. "When did that come about, Bonnie?"

"Last night. He said he was getting too old to sit a saddle for a month or more, and that it gets lonesome on a wagon seat by himself. He said I'd be company to him."

69

Zumbro took a step forward, his mouth forming another question. Then he shifted direction and headed for his horse. Without a word he stepped into the stirrup and swung up. It was a signal for everyone to move. Almost as one, the Horseshoe crew mounted and rode. Up to the hogback above the river bend, and down to the milling herd. And there Ira Borden waited, under the same post-oak where he and Bennett had talked the day before.

Bennett swung down beside him. In the East fingers of gray showed on the horizon, and the faraway sage had silver tips. The cattle were colorless shadows moving over a colorless land.

"I figure forty days on the trail," Ira Borden said. His raw-boned face was in shadow beneath his big hat, but Bennett could see the frosty eyes peering out at him.

"That's fast traveling—nearly fifteen miles a day. You're cutting it close, Borden."

Borden's broad back turned toward him. The rancher went toward his waiting horse, unwilling as usual to engage in long discussion. He said, "That's why the herd is small. I could have trailed three times this many."

Saddle leather creaked and Borden started to turn his horse back toward the camp and the supply wagon he would ride with Bonnie Gray.

Bennett's voice stopped him. "One thing, Borden," he said. "Those men are with you because they expect back wages whether they deliver this herd or not and a bonus in gold coin if they do. They're not sure they'll get to Missouri but they're counting on that gold. You've got that gold, have you?"

For a moment the bulky form in the saddle stiffened.

70

Borden kneed the bronc around, leaned over the saddle horn and spoke in a hoarse whisper.

"I'm a man of my word. Something could happen to me, but I'd want my word kept. The chuck wagon has a false floor, one laid on top of the other. Built it myself. There's a hundred and fifty double eagles between those boards, each one wrapped in a piece of burlap so they won't rattle. I put them there. They all know I've got it with me but they don't know where. See that they don't find out." Borden straightened in the saddle, and his voice lifted to its full bellow. "Now let's drive 'em north, Kell. Drive the Horseshoe north!"

A lift of the reins, a nudge of a heavy knee and Borden's horse went away from the herd. Bennett stared after him, stunned by the abruptness with which the rancher had disclosed a secret he trusted to no other man. Why had he done it? Bennett could not guess but he knew Borden had filled this trail drive with temptation. First the gold, then the sultry, dark-haired girl whom Wade Zumbro was taking to a wedding in Missouri. Bennett's job would be easier without either of them.

He had little time to ponder the mysteries of the rancher's behavior. Borden's voice had echoed across the plain, and the crew reacted.

Riders took their positions and a call as old as Texas broke the still dawn.

"Hi—ei-ei-yi!" Bert Roscoe sounded the cattle call. "Hi-ei-ei-yi!" Bennett found himself repeating it at the top of his lungs and he laughed, savoring the memories it recalled.

Restless, impatient beasts stirred. Movement ahead first, sifting down through the herd until it reached the stubborn stragglers. Toward the Trinity they moved, with Zumbro and the flankers building the point and pushing the leaders into the shallow waters. No trouble here on the home grounds, no hesitation in a herd that had waded this river before. But what of the Red, the Canadian, the Arkansas and the many other ahead? What would be the temper of the herd and the men then?

Bennett Kell said a silent prayer as he left the post-oak and put his own horse into the river.

On the fringe of the herd he passed Bert Roscoe, and the redhead grinned at him. Above the sound of milling cattle he shouted: "Won't be long now, Kell! Won't be long till you see that gal in Missouri."

"I'm willing," Bennett said, grinning. To himself he added: "But I'll have to get past Toby Rusk and the boys first."

Seven

From the upper reaches of the Trinity, over the Texas flatlands, the Horseshoe herd trailed north. A step at a time, a mile at a time. North and east they went, under a sky that was filled only with sunshine and immense distances which mocked the footsteps of man.

A few days of faltering, of annoying delays as the leaders stopped in their tracks to muzzle choice grazing spots or tried to backtrack to water. Lariats swung their monotonous circles, men shouted and cursed, and the quarter horses bobbed in and out of the bulky herd. Then the pattern was set and the herd moved along, resigned to continuous movement by day and grazing by sunset and dawn. The pattern was movement and the men were a part of the pattern.

"Swing men, away from the brush! Drag men, close 'em up! Shoot the quitter, we gotta eat beef, anyway!" Bennett circled the herd with his orders, his plainsman's eyes forever touching the bobbing beasts and the trail ahead.

He treated the herd as his own and the men accepted

it. He saw little of Ira Borden during the first days on the trail and he was not sure whether he should accept the rancher's inattentiveness as a compliment to himself or put it down as a reason for worry.

Borden still rode the supply wagon and as the drive shaped up each morning he was joined on the high spring seat by Bonnie Gray. To allow her privacy, Borden had permitted the girl to bunk in the wagon ever since they left the Trinity. And Bennett noticed that the rancher spread his own blankets just a few paces beyond the rear wheels of the vehicle each night.

During the day Borden ranged ahead with Cass Bailey's chuck wagon, the two of them selecting each evening's bedding ground. Since his fight with Zumbro the girl had avoided Bennett, but she joined Zumbro at the campfire for a while each evening. Although Zumbro showed no open animosity toward Bennett, the man had as little to do with him as possible. Zumbro was a skilled rider, a good man with cattle, and he did his job well. But when Bennett joined him at point occasionally, Zumbro drifted away to the edge of the herd.

For the most part Bennett kept his mind on the herd and its vital importance to him. But the relationship among Zumbro, Borden and the girl was a part of this, and their behavior kept creeping into his thoughts. That night on the Trinity he'd been sure Bonnie Gray shared Wade Zumbro's hatred for the Horseshoe owner. What had changed her mind? And why had Borden, who had openly disapproved the girl's presence on the drive, suddenly become friendly and attentive to her?

Bennett rode with a nagging feeling that something was amiss.

74

He was sure of it a week later, on a morning when he fell from his saddle in a dead faint after a troublesome crossing over a fork of the Sabine River. The ragged gash in his left shoulder had given him trouble from the time Wade Zumbro's spur rowel ripped his flesh, but he had not guessed its seriousness. For the last two days he'd gritted his teeth against pain and nausea, but he did not suspect that the poison of it was eating into his system and sapping his strength until the ground lurched suddenly up at him and he lost his senses.

When he regained consciousness, Cass Bailey was standing over him and Bonnie Gray was kneeling at his side.

Cass said, "You can stop fussing over him now, ma'am. He's going to be all right."

Bonnie rose, and Bennett gave a start at her striking appearance. She was dressed in a soft fawn-colored riding skirt of fine doeskin. An expensive yellow satin shirt was tucked into the wasp waist, accentuating the swell of her breasts and sending fiery flecks into her almond eyes. She stood with her hands folded in front of her, gazing down on him with a smile quirking the corners of her lips.

"I'm glad to see that look in your eyes, Bennett," she said lightly. "When you can look at a woman like that you're as good as new."

Aside from a throbbing ache in his shoulder and a burning sensation across his scalp, Bennett felt strong enough. He forced a dry chuckle. "Thought I was out of my head with fever there for a minute. Saw something like you on a calendar in a bar down on the Brazos one time, and I thought I was back there."

A flush crept up from Bonnie's slender neck to stain

her olive cheeks. "You go to hell," she hissed through set teeth, and turned away, teasing him with her hips as she went.

"You take it easy there, Kell. Ride in the wagon with Cass for a while."

It was Ira Borden's voice booming at him across the open spaces. Bennett turned his head and saw the supply wagon twenty yards away. Solid and erect on the seat was Ira Borden, waiting patiently for Bonnie to join him. A rough palm reached for soft, slender fingers and Borden helped the girl up beside him.

She leaned close, placed her hand on a brawny shoulder, and said something in Borden's ear. A rare, roaring laugh broke over hard, thin lips and Borden threw his massive head back and guffawed. He slapped the girl on the thigh, clucked to the horses, and the wagon rolled.

"Come along, Cass. We gotta pass that herd, you know."

"Like you say, Ira. Like you say!" Cass Bailey's voice was a high, nervous quaver when he raised it to volume. He eyed the wagon a moment, then turned his head and spat on the grass.

"Damn Ira Borden's black soul," Cass said in a thick whisper. "It's the first time in twenty years I've knowed how to hate him."

Bennett sat up experimentally, keeping his hands braced on the ground behind him. Bright spots danced before his eyes. A bandage was wrapped slantwise under his armpit and tied on the side of his neck. Over the wound on his shoulder blade was a damp, mushy pad and he knew Cass had made a grain poultice to draw out the infection.

"You upset about the girl, Cass?"

The balding cook's skinny hands hung limply at his side, fingers twitching. His tiny, dancing eyes swung out over the plain and back to Bennett. "The girl and them clothes she's wearing," Cass said. "Them's Mary Borden's finest things, the ones Ira aimed to cart to Missouri and take to her on the railroad. Now he's put 'em on that hussy. It ain't decent, Kell. Mary Borden was a good wife to Ira till the trouble came."

A scowl pinched at Bennett's dark face as the meaning of Cass Bailey's words became clear to him. Strange that it had never occurred to him that Borden was married, that he had not always been a bitter, raw-tempered old man who stomped and prowled across the earth like a lone gray wolf.

Now he remembered that Borden had seemed impressed that first day with the answer to a single question: "What made you pull out of the gangs up north, Kell?" Bennett had replied, "A woman," and Borden had seemed pleased.

Cass Bailey's taut voice cut through his thoughts. "What do you make of it, Kell?"

Rising, Bennett leaned against the wagon wheel and shook his head. He wanted to put the cook's words out of his mind, but he knew the man was genuinely concerned and his own curiosity was needling him.

"You could make a lot of things out of it, Cass," he said at last. "A man Ira's age can get taken by the sight of a frisky young female more often than not. Or you could say Bonnie is just aggravating Wade Zumbro and Borden's doing the same. That little filly likes a winner. She told me that herself. And you got to admit there's few men who could get the best of Ira Borden."

"Maybe. But one woman did, and another might. Ira ain't been the same since his wife pulled stakes on him a couple of years back. Ira swore he wouldn't give in to her, but that's what he did when he gathered this herd and headed north. His plans are to catch a train east to Boston with this last stake in his pocket and never come back."

"That the trouble you spoke of?"

"That's it. Wife trouble." Cass Bailey plucked a wisp of sage and chewed at it thoughtfully. "Ira's son Dave got killed in the war, and Mary Borden blamed Ira and hated Texas for it. Dave wasn't really old enough to fight, but Ira was so dead set on the Confederacy winning out that he lied to help get Dave into the ruckus. When word come that Dave was dead, Mary said she couldn't stand the sight of Texas no more. She wanted Ira to pull up and go back to Boston, where they come from back in forty-two, but Ira wouldn't go. So she went without him. Lord knows how, but she made it."

With an exasperated sigh Cass clambered up on the wagon. "We'll roll now if you feel up to it. Looks like your fever has about broke."

Bennett joined him on the seat, relieved that he could not feel the gash in his shoulder break open and drain as it had so many times recently. The early-morning sun was already a shaft of blazing fire against them, casting long shadows through the sage and in the washes that speared toward the river.

Bennett's gaze stayed on the wagon, and he could picture the two figures sitting close on the seat, hidden from view by the canvas sheet over the bows. A strange resentment rose in him as he recalled Borden's gnarled

78

hand slapping at the girl's rounded thigh, and the thought flashed through his mind that a man as old and dried out as Borden had no right to such intimacy with a woman as young and desirable as Bonnie. He cursed under his breath and fumbled in his shirt pocket for the stub of a cigar. Hell, he told himself bitterly, I'm beginning to think like a jealous man!

They rode in silence for a time, Bennett finding contentment in his cigar and Cass Bailey worried and preoccupied. But the cook's mood wore off finally and he began to talk of the ambitions that lie deep inside all men.

After studying Bennett with guarded glances for a few minutes, he said, "I'm sure hoping you're as good a man as you claim. I sure hope you take this herd through to Missouri. If you do, I'm taking my stake and heading back to Texas and buy up the Horseshoe. I've got me a chance now, the only one I've had in my whole life."

"Borden's giving up the Horseshoe?"

"Yeah. Like I mentioned, he's going back East to his wife. He left the Horseshoe in charge of a lawyer in Crosscut to sell to whoever'd take it at whatever they could pay whenever."

Cass's bony face sobered with concern again. "That was his plan when he started north. Maybe it's been changed now by that half-breed filly. One thing I can't figure, Kell, is why Zumbro don't shoot off his mouth about this deal. Zumbro's mean, that I know. It ain't because he's afraid of Ira. Damn, I got a feeling I ain't ever going to see Missouri nor the Horseshoe again."

Bennett took a deep drag on the cigar and let the smoke waft slowly up past dark, squinted eyes. "You'll see Missouri, Cass," he said quietly. "That's one thing nobody's going to stop—not Bonnie Gray or Ira Borden or Zumbro."

Cass studied his face for a long moment, apparently gaining assurance from the set of Bennett's jaws and the calm intensity of the black eyes. "Then maybe we could team up, son," he said hopefully. "The Horseshoe has still got cattle on it. If we can drive one herd to Missouri, we can drive another. Next time, we'll have the whole state of Texas behind us."

"I couldn't do that, Cass. Next time I'll be driving my own—from the Brazos. I've got my own place. But I've got to deliver this herd first. A big man told me once that folks would forget I was ever on the wrong side if I could do something that would help other people enough. Delivering the Horseshoe to the railhead will help keep a railroad building, help the state of Texas— and me."

Cass nodded. "Sounds like a pretty smart man."

"He's an important man. He's the guardian of the woman I aim to marry, and he doesn't figure I'm worthy of her unless I can drive this herd right down the throats of the border gangs."

"So that's it," Cass grunted, shaking his head in wonder. "Sometimes it looks like a woman's got her hands on the reins that drive the whole world."

"I figure you're just about right, Cass."

And as Bennett spoke his thoughts went to Bonnie again. He was sure that in some way her hands were clutching for a grip on the reins which guided the actions of Ira Borden, and there was danger in how she might handle them.

80

Eight

They camped at Willow Spring that night and the drudgery of the drive was beginning to tell on the men. Around the campfire they were silent and morose and Scrap Dooley began to complain about Cass Bailey's food.

At another time it might have passed as a joke. But Cass had lost faith in a man this day, and it had worked a change in him. Without warning he turned and flung a panful of soggy corn batter at Scrap Dooley. It missed his face but a spot of it splattered his shoulder and Scrap was on his feet, shouting curses.

He took a step toward the cook, fist cocked, and Cass raised a big tin bucket, ready to swing it by the bail.

From the shadows behind Cass, Borden said, "Back up and sit down, Scrap. Cass cooks what he has."

There was a crackle in the rumbling voice. Scrap Dooley stood poised a moment, and his eyes went to the leathery face in the shadows. Slowly his skinny fists relaxed and he sat down.

A sheepish grin spread over his face. He glanced aside at Bennett, "I reckon I had it coming," he murmured, and began to build a smoke.

Before the two men came to blows Bennett would have taken a hand himself, but he had been preoccupied in the moment when Ira Borden spoke. He had been watching Bonnie.

She had sprung to her feet, her eyes wild with expectation. Her slender body was aquiver, as though fired by passion, and she was hugging her breasts with folded arms. She found Bennett watching her and a light leaped in her eyes as their glances met. A smile touched her lips and she turned away, walking into the shadows of the bushes which grew along the spring.

A voice beside Bennett said musingly, "Notice how Shad Miller's been feasting his eyes on her all evening? I'll lay you four to one he follers her."

It was Ben Lufton, the boss wrangler, speaking in his soft drawl. Bennett said nothing, but he looked at Shad Miller, the cotton-topped kid from the Big Bend. Barely twenty but there was a war behind him, a thin saber scar on the point of his cheek and an air of deviltry in his quick smile.

Shad's head swung to follow Bonnie's graceful figure and the tip of his tongue darted across his lips. He rose, tilted his dusty hat rakishly and stepped across the tongue of the chuck wagon. He was a little too casual in his manner to be convincing. He took three steps toward the spring before Bennett said, "Don't go over there, Shad," and he wished immediately that he had kept still.

Somebody snickered and Shad Miller's face turned

82

blood-red. Then silence, and other glances lifted to the shadows concealing Bonnie Gray. It was as though a curtain had been lifted, baring men's innermost thoughts, and there was no longer a need for pretenses.

A moody silence hung over the camp, unbroken until Wade Zumbro rose to get his night horse from the remuda. He stalked across the darkening plain and said, "It's nighthawking time, and you and me come first, Shad."

There was a raw, hard-reined fury in Zumbro's tone and in the hard crunch of his boots. Shad Miller hesitated, eyeing Zumbro's muscular back. He got up slowly, hitching at his gunbelt, and fell in step behind Zumbro with the wariness of a man marching to a duel.

"You sure lit a fuse that time," Ben Lufton murmured, and walked off with a sigh, seeming to regret his part in the incident.

Bennett could find no reason to blame the wizened wrangler. The fuse had been lighted the first time Bonnie rolled her almond eyes and flounced her skirt at the Horseshoe crew. But now the explosion was imminent, and Bennett was gripped by a cold, futile anger because he was powerless to prevent it.

As he rolled up in his borrowed blankets he was struck by the hope that weariness would hold the men in check. He had not rejoined the herd until noon, but even a half-day in the saddle had left his muscles limp and his spine aching from the constant jostle of the saddle. Part of his own fatigue was due to the shoulder wound, but the best man could not swallow dust, hold a horse in tow and be alert to the movement of cattle for twelve hours without needing rest.

Presently Bonnie walked back through the camp and Bennett saw her silhouetted briefly against the light from the fire. He studied her through half-closed eyes, then turned his head away with a curse. She was inviting trouble, and when it came it could ruin Bennett Kell. Here, in a brawl over a woman, the Horseshoe drive could fall apart. And when it did Bennett would be back where he started—a cattle thief who salved his conscience with the excuse that he was avenging a wrong.

Ragged gray clouds sliding in from the southeast hung low over the Horseshoe camp. In the distance a coyote complained about the murky night, and nearby the dying embers of the fire sizzled and crackled.

One of the sounds had awakened him, Bennett thought. He lay a moment without moving, his senses alert.

Then he heard the voices, low-pitched and secretive. He eased up on his elbow, swinging his glance around the sleeping camp. From the bed grounds, two hundred yards away, he could hear the high tenor voice of Shad Miller crooning to the cattle. This meant it was not yet midnight, for the second shift of nighthawks had not yet replaced Miller and Zumbro.

While he waited for the voices again, Bennett slipped into his boots and stood up. He buckled on his gunbelt and looked around the gloomy camp. His glance touched the canvas sheet of the supply wagon, parked midway between the bunched horses and the fire. A board squeaked, and even in the darkness he could see the vehicle sway as a result of some movement inside. He went swiftly toward it, his pulse hammering furiously.

"Get out! Get out and leave me alone!" Bonnie Gray's voice was a hissing whisper, but it carried clearly in the still night.

And the reply came in the croaking tones Ira Borden used for a whisper. "I'm here now and I'll have what I want before I go. You asked me here, girl. Now you shut up and give in or I'll set you off on a horse to find your way back!"

Bennett's steps lengthened. He was almost at the tailgate when the tussle started in earnest. Quick-shifting feet rocked the wagon, and one side of the canvas cover ballooned outward as a body lunged against it. There was the sound of a hand slapping flesh, and then a faint cry from Bonnie.

"Please, Ira." Her voice was full-toned and husky now, but it held a note of desperation. "There'll be another time. When—when it's safer."

"No." A single word, still guarded, from Borden. And the wagon swayed again.

The girl's scream was loud and piercing, rising with the sound of tearing cloth. Mingled with the scream were the curses of a frustrated man.

Bennett stopped in his tracks, his first thought going to the blankets that would be thrown aside behind him and of men piling to their feet in alarm. As he stood there, Bonnie came out of the wagon in a hurtling leap that cleared the tailgate and brought her into the open behind the vehicle. She landed on her feet a few yards in front of him and for a moment he could only stare at her in amazement. She waved her arms to catch her balance, her eyes looking wildly about for a place of refuge.

She saw Bennett, and a little cry of relief broke from her lips. And then as she threw herself into his arms Bennett realized why her sudden appearance had stunned him so completely. A shred of ruffled blue cloth, apparently part of a night dress, hung around the girl's neck, and part of one sleeve was bunched around her wrist. Otherwise Bonnie was naked.

Her pointed breasts pressed against his shirt and Bennett could feel the warmth of her arms around his neck as she clung to him, sobbing into his ear. And over her shoulder he saw the wild face of Ira Borden, thin lips drawn back over hard, even teeth, iron-gray hair bristling on his hatless head.

Tearing the girl's arms from his neck, Bennett pushed her toward the front of the wagon. "Pull a blanket out of the stores and cover yourself." And to Ira Borden: "You damn fool, you can explain this to the crew yourself!"

Borden stepped to the ground. He set his hand on the cedar butt of the holstered Colt and, his face settling into familiar lines, said calmly, "I'm a fool, yes. But I don't explain anything to anybody in this crew. My home is where these cattle move, and in my home I don't explain my behavior to those who work for me."

Almost without thinking Bennett placed his own hand on the bone handle of the gun at his side. He felt contempt for this rawboned old man who tried to take a woman by force and he wanted to strike out at the calm, immobile face. But the voice of reason held him back. There would be fighting enough for all of them before they reached the railhead and it would be foolish to spend themselves over a woman who had invited trouble.

With a shrug he turned away. And as he did so he came face to face with Wade Zumbro.

Zumbro stood less than six feet away, his face hidden in the shadow of his hat brim. But the glitter of Zumbro's eyes cut through the shadows and the sound of his breath wheezing through his nostrils held the warning of a snake's rattle. On widespread legs, shoulders hunched forward, an arm crooked above his gun, Wade Zumbro stood and glared at Ira Borden.

"I'm going to kill you, Ira." Zumbro's voice was low-toned, almost sad. "I had a hunch about this, so I pulled away from the herd. And I was right. I was only a dozen steps behind Kell all the way here. I'm going to kill you for what you did, Ira."

"I did nothing," Ira Borden growled. "She asked me to come to the wagon. She asked me to come after the boys turned in and before you finished your riding trick. What do you make of that?"

"We're wasting time, Ira. Pull that gun, and don't try to walk off this time. I don't care where the bullet lands if you don't."

A deep breath swelled Borden's chest. He let the air out slowly, his expression unchanging. "She's rubbed all over me for days and tonight she started out by grabbing me and kissing me. I've been a long time without a woman and a man stands for just so much of that. But that wasn't what brought it to—to this, Zumbro. She wanted to make a bargain. She wanted me to show her my gold first. I meant to teach her a lesson."

When Ira Borden stopped talking Zumbro's lips twisted bitterly.

He said, "I'm slapping leather, Ira," and his hand jabbed at the holstered gun. Down and up, almost too fast to see, a hand driven by the fury of an offended lover lifted the gun.

Flame and shot showered the air and Wade Zumbro was whirled in a half-circle and slammed against the ground. Blood seeped between the fingers Zumbro clutched to his shoulder, and he turned a look of pained surprise upon Bennett Kell.

"I work for Borden," Bennett said to him. "I want to keep him alive until we reach Kansas City."

At the corner of the wagon, where he had stopped when the argument started, Bennett Kell's black eyes smoldered with the deadliness of the powder smoke wafting from the gun in his hand. A short distance away, where they'd drawn up abruptly when the gunplay started, stood the men of the Horseshoe crew.

Bennett said to them, "Give Zumbro a hand."

The men moved in and Bennett looked at Ira Borden. In the years since he had come from the East, Borden had become as a part of this raw and rugged land. It was likely that he had perfected his gunspeed as thoroughly as he had his skill with cattle and horses. But when Bennett drew and fired, Borden had not yet bothered to reach for his gun.

"That girl was after my gold," Borden said angrily. "I'd guess she and Zumbro had this whole thing planned."

"Gold has a way of drawing thieves," Bennett said.

The rancher drew himself up tall, his gray eyes cold and defiant. "You're thinking I stole it myself. My father was a shipbuilder in Boston. He died and left me three thousand in gold. I took it and headed for Texas, figuring to build with it. But I got a good start and never had to touch it, and I've saved it to this day. I've been hard. I had to be to make it out here. But I'm no thief, Kell."

"Sorry," Bennett murmured. He'd wanted to hear about the gold, and he'd jabbed at Borden's conscience deliberately. Now he regretted his action and he felt he had lost stature in the exchange.

Borden kept staring at him, his face thoughtful. "You could have beaten Zumbro that first day," Borden said after a moment. "I was a fool to think I saved your life."

"Maybe. But you trusted me and I needed that worse."

Borden's lips clamped tight, indicating he had nothing more to say. But Bennett stood where he was, a look of challenge on his face. Borden moved off toward his bed. With a glance at Bennett, he snatched his blankets from the ground and moved them far away from their usual place near the wagon.

As Bennett started toward the campfire, Bonnie called to him. He whirled, surprised that she had passed so swiftly out of his mind. Bonnie had re-entered the wagon from the front. Now she was on her knees at the tailgate, facing him with a hand clutching a blanket under her chin.

"Thanks, Bennett," she called and as she lifted the

hand to wave to him the blanket parted and slipped off her shoulders. In the instant before she could recover the blanket, stray beams of light from the replenished fire glinted on her naked shoulders and full breasts. The sight of her stirred him with desire and his stride faltered. Then he walked on, his steps faster. If he went back to her it would no longer matter whether he reached Missouri or not.

Nine

Strips torn from flour sacks, grain poultices and boiling water were the things a man patched his wounds with on the trail. Cass Bailey made use of them while he worked on Wade Zumbro's shoulder, cleaning, daubing and binding it tight. And when he had finished his darting eyes found Bennett lounging in the shadows.

Cass said, "That was a good clean shot. In the front, out the back. Them kind git sore but not nasty. He'll be fit in a day or two."

Grunting, Cass rose and began gathering up his utensils as calmly as if he had been baking biscuits. A man on his feet was in good health and gunfire was serious only when it was fatal.

Slowly, his face still molded in angry lines, Bennett stepped into the firelight. His quick plainsman's glance swung over the lounging crew and the men fell back to make a path for him.

Clay Macklin stood and stretched elaborately, looking around at Ben Lufton and the others with a significant glance. "Them cows will be walking again at daybreak, and I aim to feel at least as good as them critters do." He yawned and headed for his blankets, and the others drifted away with him.

Beyond the fire Wade Zumbro sat as he had while Cass Bailey treated his wound. He had stripped off his blood-smeared shirt. Now he sat clenching and balling it in the fist of his good arm. Firelight glistened on the rippling muscles of his heavy shoulders, and Bennett could read the man's inner turmoil in the tension of his body.

"Borden thinks you and Bonnie had that whole thing planned," he said bluntly.

"What could I gain by it?"

Zumbro kept his head down but his voice was thick with bridled fury. Bennett moved around to squat on his heels, his eyes prying at the man's face.

"Let's not string this out, Zumbro. You could come up on Borden like that and scare him out of a pile of gold if the cards fell right. Another man might have paid off to keep you quiet—or to save his life. Borden figures that's what Bonnie has been building him up to."

"Maybe she has. It takes a man a long time to learn all there is to know about a woman. But I wasn't in it, Kell."

Jaws clenched, face pale with pain, Wade Zumbro paused and hitched at the bandage on his shoulder. He flung the wadded shirt away from him and looked directly at Bennett for the first time.

"Maybe I ought to thank you, Kell," he murmured. "Maybe you stopped something that should have been stopped. But I just don't cotton to a man who puts a slug in me."

"Me neither," Bennett said. "That's why I want you to pull out of this outfit. You can sit a horse. Head for Kansas City and wait for the herd to come in. You have my word you'll get paid when we get there. This thing is going to stay between us and I don't have time for it. I don't have time to watch these cows and watch for the minute you'll feel like reaching for your gun again."

Zumbro pushed to his feet. Sweat glistened on his handsome face and the muscles of his chest bunched themselves in knots.

"Pay me, Kell. Pay me and I'll take Bonnie and pull out."

"You're being contrary," Bennett said. He stood up slowly. "Borden won't open that gold until he sees the loading pens. He can't afford to and you know it. But you have my word."

"I want my wages. And until I get them, I aim to stay close to Ira Borden. There's no guarantee any of us will see Kansas City. But some time, some way, I aim to have what's coming to me. The way I figure it, there ain't much you can do about that, Kell."

Again Wade Zumbro's gaze lifted directly to Bennett's face. For a moment their eyes locked, reckless blue against flinty black. At last Bennett shrugged and turned away without replying.

Behind him, Zumbro's voice leaped out in a defiant whisper. "You needn't worry about my gun, Kell. If I grab for it, I'll holler first."

Bennett went on in silence, not daring to give voice to the anger boiling within him. For a long time afterward he lay in his blankets wide-eyed and sleepless, pondering the new tensions the night had created.

Bert Roscoe and Monte Cole came out of the shadows presently and went toward the remuda, ready to take their turn with the herd. As they passed near him, Bennett sat up and beckoned to Roscoe.

The red-haired puncher hunkered beside him, his freckled face creased with a half-grin. "Hell of a night to be going to a dance," he said.

For a man like Bert Roscoe life ran in simple channels. He laughed at himself, laughed at the world and managed to stay on the fringe of life's complex problems. But at the moment Bennett ignored the man's wry humor.

He said, "Tell Shad Miller where the shot came from. He's probably sitting out there wrung dry with curiosity about it. I don't want him asking me a lot of questions, so tell him about it."

"Shad won't ask no questions," Roscoe grunted. "I figure you settled that trouble for good. Me, I aim to look at nothing except what I see popping up between my horse's ears."

Every man of the Horseshoe crew was not cast from the same mold as Bert Roscoe, but Bennett gained comfort from the man's words. He had seen the change in the men when he returned to the campfire and he told himself the incident at the wagon had served one useful purpose. For the present there would be no problem with Bonnie Gray. The men had seen the kind of trouble a woman could cause among them and they wanted no part of it.

But what about Wade Zumbro? His face troubled, Bennett fumbled in his saddlebags and withdrew one of the cigars he had bought for just such moments as this.

He needed to remember the things he'd seen in Missouri, needed to think of Ada's beauty and Big Jim McKittridge's success. It was a craving for these things that had brought him here, and they must take him back.

Around him the plain was dark and still again. A faint breeze blew in from the bedding grounds, bringing with it the mingled odors of sage and dust and cattle droppings. Bennett gazed about him at the sleeping camp, breathing a silent hope that daylight would witness the same solitude.

He let the rich cigar smoke trail slowly through his nostrils, recalling the night he had sat and smoked with McKittridge. But tonight this symbolic gesture brought him little relief. With Wade Zumbro and Ira Borden so close, Kansas City and Ada seemed an impossible distance away.

Presently he put out the cigar and returned to his blankets, determined to be rested and alert when tomorrow came. He heard Shad Miller come in from the herd and fall instantly asleep. And afterward Monte Cole began a mournful nightherding song, making up words as cowboys always do:

> It's a long way to Missouri . . .
> Over trails where others died.
> It's a long way to Missouri,
> Git along, cow, durn your hide . . .

On and on went the song, and Monte seemed never to run out of words. For a while Bennett listened, and before he was asleep he knew much of the worries which Monte Cole carried in his mind. They were not unlike the problems which worried Bennett Kell.

A night passed, a day was born and the hidden sun threw its first drab light over the immense land. Yesterday was dead, a forgotten thing, and there was no mention of the flare-up of the night before.

But Cass Bailey's pots rattled louder, the men talked more and the usual moment of stillness fell over the crew when Ira Borden strode in to have his breakfast.

Back erect, shoulders squared, Borden stood near the fire and let his eyes run over the faces around him. Bonnie Gray, clad in flannel shirt and levis now, lifted a thin hand expectantly to her cheek. Borden looked past her as though she were a scrub pine. At last he turned toward Bennett. "I see you've still got Zumbro with us."

Bennett nodded. "When I fire a man, I pay him. I'm not carrying any money on me, Ira."

Borden nodded, glanced casually at Zumbro's sullen face. "Get you a shirt from the wagon, Zumbro. I'd hate to see a man survive a bullet and die of sunstroke. Ride the wagon today. When you feel up to it, fork your saddle again. You'll be paid in Missouri."

It was a warning to them all. Borden meant to hold to his gold until he collected for his cattle. Payday would come in Missouri, no matter what other compromises had to be made.

In the center of the lounging circle Borden took his seat and ate his food. He wanted them to be aware of his presence, to be reminded that he was a solid force among them. And as the rim of the sun peeped over the horizon, Borden rose and washed his plate. To Cass Bailey, he said, "You should have been a doctor, Cass. You never was much of a cook."

And to Bennett: "I'll ride point with you today, Kell. I expect to camp on the Red River three days from now."

Like men answering a call to arms, the Horseshoe crew followed Ira Borden's long strides to the remuda. They roped their best horses, broncs with solid barrels and a lot of bottom. Horses sure of foot and long on wind; horses to meet the challenge of a man like Ira Borden.

Sixty miles to the Red River, and Ira Borden expected to be there in three days! Bennett had kept the men posted as they moved along, and they knew what they faced. Across the sand flats, over the rolling hills, through scrub pine and rock patches they would have to ride like demons or watch their hard pride wither under an old man's stare.

There was no time for talk, no time to make trouble or worry about it. Borden rode at point, pacing the leaders, stretching the herd out and daring the drag riders to close it up. Salt crusted on a man's beard, and dirt etched the lines of his face. Even the sun rested first now, sinking under the blue hills of the west while the herd moved on through the dusk and under the starshine.

"Who in hell is he mad at?" Clay Macklin murmured wearily as he turned his horse over to Ben Lufton at the rope corral. "Two days of this and everybody's dead but him. Who's he mad at?"

A dozen feet away, rubbing gently at the coat of his dun mount, Bennett Kell kept his head down and ignored the question.

But Ben Lufton took it up. "Maybe he ain't mad at nobody," the wrangler drawled. "Maybe he's just scared."

"Scared of what?"

"Of himself. That Bonnie gal is the kind to get a grip on a man. Maybe Ira wants to get to Missouri and head East to his wife fast as he can. Maybe he's afraid if he don't do that she'll be able to make her own terms next time."

Clay Macklin raised his glance and stared at Ben Lufton. Then he moved off toward the chuck wagon with a hardspoken "Damn—"

Bennett finished caring for his horse and started in the same direction. The wrangler fell in step beside him. Behind them came the sound of running feet, and they turned together, both startled, both alert.

It was Shad Miller, hat in hand, his long blond hair dangling in his eyes. Despite the pumping of his long legs, the youngster's movement was slow, his knees wobbly with fatigue.

"What is it?" Bennett asked worriedly.

Shad shook his head. "Just wanted to catch up," he said breathlessly. "Just wanted to tell you something."

"What is it?"

"Today's the Fourth of July, Bennett! I been keeping count. Know what that means?"

Bennett let his breath out slowly, his mind running back swiftly in search of the time when holidays had ceased to have a special meaning for him. But here on the trail, a thousand miles from nowhere, Shad Miller had taken the trouble to remember and Bennett found himself longing for his own youth.

98

He said quietly, "You tell me about it, Shad. What does it mean?"

"Why it means I'll have a birthday exactly one month from today. I'll be twenty-one."

Chuckling to himself, Shad went on ahead of them, eager to boast to the others of the day he would become a man. For the first time in days, Bennett permitted himself a smile. This would be something for Shad Miller to tell his grandchildren about: He became a man on the trail to Missouri!

Suddenly he was thoughtful again. From the start of the drive, the Horseshoe crew had been pushing toward an inevitable fight. Only he knew this, for only he knew that Toby Rusk and Wally Bryan had warned him not to return to Missouri. A youngster like Shad Miller could lose his life against ruffians like Rusk and Bryan, and Bennett would bear the responsibility.

Beside him Ben Lufton said quietly, "While you been riding yourself ragged the past two days, Zumbro has been getting plenty of rest on the wagon with his girl. That would give him a big edge if he started something."

A scowl pinched at Bennett's face, and he gave the wizened wrangler a sidelong glance. "You worry too much, Ben."

"Not exactly. I just wanted to get your mind turned off of what it was on just now. I didn't like the look on your face."

Bennett flexed his left shoulder unconsciously, feeling for the first time in days a dull ache under the scars left by Zumbro's spur. He found the wrangler watching him and swore silently. Ben Lufton had succeeded in influencing his thoughts.

He had more important things to worry about than Shad Miller's future. And the most urgent of these, he reflected, was keeping himself alive.

Old Ben Lufton's words came back to him in the middle of the night, and Bennett found himself snapping instantly awake. Weariness was a throbbing ache through his body, but he could not sleep. He lay rigidly still, his ears straining for some foreign sound in the night. And almost without thinking he sent his gaze searching over the camp until he located the sleeping form of Wade Zumbro.

All was as it should be. The heavy breathing of bone-tired men stirred the air, and the crooning voices of the nighthawks came like a lonely lullaby from the herd. But still he lay awake and stared into the star-jeweled sky, bothered by a sense of foreboding and a feeling that the peace of the night would not last.

He dozed fitfully through the night, and was up as soon as Cass Bailey punched up the breakfast fire. While the crew ate, Bennett sat aside in watchful silence. He kept Wade Zumbro always in sight, wondering if this would be the day of final settlement, but after breakfast had passed without incident, he shrugged off his fears. The men trooped away from the wagons to saddle their horses. Wade Zumbro was still sullen and uncommunicative, and occasionally he gave Bennett a sidelong glance filled with hate. But he kept his hand away from his gun and was among the first to lift his saddle to begin the day's work.

Bennett was reaching for his own saddle when the first three shots shattered the stillness of dawn. He straightened, his thoughts going again to Zumbro. He squinted anxiously in the direction of the remuda, saw the crew running back in alarm.

Ira Borden's booming voice brought him spinning around. Beyond the rancher's towering form, Bennett saw six charging horsemen. They were gray and ghostly figures in the colorless dawn, but the fire that streaked from their hands with each exploding shot sent death sweeping ahead of them.

"Cut them down!" Ira Borden was shouting. "Cut them down before they get to the cattle!"

Borden's right hand blurred with speed, and the big cedar-butted Colt roared an answer to the attack. Bennett, marveling at the swiftness of the rancher's draw, reached for his own gun.

The acrid smell of powder smoke sifted over the camp as the Horseshoe crew opened fire. Bullets dug up dust beyond the parked wagons, falling short of their mark by several yards. Bennett scowled, pondering the reason for the attack. The attackers were out of Texas, not from the vengeful lands to the north; they rode the wiry mustangs of the range country, and they had the natural grace of men who made their living astride a horse. And as they came closer, Bennett saw that some of them wore the gray shirts and turned-up hats which had been a part of the uniform of the Confederate army.

A break occurred in the charging line. One of the horsemen grabbed at a shoulder, reeled in the saddle and fell to the ground. The others wheeled in a rearing circle, going back to the fallen man. Booted feet scuffed up dust while they dragged the wounded man to cover behind an outcropping of gray rock. Then the attackers were all on their feet, diving for cover as Ira Borden screamed for the Horseshoe crew to increase their fire.

101

Bennett Kell lowered his gun. He ripped off his faded yellow neck scarf, knotted it around the gun barrel, and waved it over his head as a flag of truce. Ira Borden spun in his tracks, catching the movement from the corner of his eye, and a knobby hand reached for the gun.

"Hand me that, you fool!" Borden's voice was low-pitched, grating like sandpaper on rock. "Seems a man has to watch you every minute when the going gets rough. I'll leave every mother's son of that gang a corpse before I'll look over my shoulder for them from here to Missouri. Hand me that flag, I say! There'll be no surrender while I'm alive!"

"Get the blood out of your eye, Borden." Bennett's face was solemn, reflecting a strange regret. "I'm not giving in to them. All I want is a chance to talk things over before somebody gets killed. We may find that's a friend of yours out there."

Ira Borden shook his head. He took another step toward Bennett, his breath wheezing angrily in his chest. The grip tightened on his heavy gun, and he weighed it in his hand like a club. Bennett tensed, trying to read the rancher's intentions by the set of Borden's bear-trap mouth, and he thought, *Here's where he'll try spitting on me.*

"Somebody's coming this way, Ira!" Cass Bailey's squeaking voice was as sharp as though he were calling for help. He had heard Borden's command to Bennett Kell, had seen the challenge rise in the younger man's face, and his pinched face had filled with dread.

Quiet seconds ticked past while Ira Borden continued to glare at Bennett. Then slowly he swung around to look across the plain. The man coming

102

toward the camp was square-shouldered and stocky. A broad-brimmed hat shielded his face, but he walked with the determined gait of a man on a mission.

Borden said, "You can pull up there, mister, and I'll come out and talk." He hesitated as Bennett started forward with him, turned as if to object, then went silently on.

"My God, Ira, is that you?" The man's voice held a note of unbelief. "Hell, I thought I was doing you a favor. Figured you was dead, or I never would have rode in like this."

A yard in front of the man, Borden stopped and braced his feet. He ran his eyes over the worn levis, the hide vest, the seamed, bewildered face. "Who're you?" he asked bluntly.

"Nat Rickard. We ain't met often, but I've seen you here and there. I run a place just above yours on the Trinity."

"And you thought I pushed some of your cattle north with mine? You ain't fighting Indians, Rickard. Don't you ever shoot at me and ask questions afterward. You won't find me so patient again."

Nat Rickard ignored Ira Borden's growling voice. His pale eyes were on Bennett's face and his mouth twisted in a bitter sneer.

"I knew you had a killer with you," Rickard said softly. "I figured by now he'd shot you in the back and turned your herd over to the thieving bastards he rides with in Missouri. It took me three days to place him, but his face stuck in my mind. He stopped at my place to ask about you, and I couldn't forget his face. When it finally come to me, I spent a day roundin' up some help."

103

Bennett Kell met the man's accusing eyes with shame and guilt needling his conscience. But he was not surprised. Suspicion had left a brooding light in Rickard's eyes that day on the Trinity, and he was the kind of man who would not forget a wrong.

Keeping his eyes on Bennett, Rickard talked to Ira Borden from the side of his mouth. He told of his own drive to Missouri; told of the ruthless attack as soon as he touched the border; told of a final effort to get the remnants of the herd to the railhead only to be thwarted by a "crazy Texan" who took the rest of the cattle.

"So you see why I rode in with my gun out," Rickard concluded angrily. "They took me by surprise and I aimed to give this skunk a dose of his own medicine. That was the only chance we had."

Borden waved his arm impatiently. "I fight my own fights, Rickard. You and your men are welcome to join me at regular wages. You can do that or stay out of my sight and out of my business. Right now, I've got a herd to move."

The creases around Nat Rickard's wide mouth thinned with anger. "We figure to go back to Texas, Borden, and put a herd on the trail. If we don't find your bones on the way, we'll follow you to the railhead. You're no better man than me. But I don't aim to leave until I get what I want."

"What's that?" Borden snapped.

Nat Rickard's thumb jabbed at Bennett Kell. "Him."

"You just got through cussing him out. What do you want with him?"

"We aim to hang him," Nat Rickard replied, and the tone of his voice indicated he expected no argument.

104

A nod from Ira Borden would settle the matter. Nat Rickard had the first claim on Bennett Kell, and in that time and place his request was not unreasonable. Across the unsettled wilderness of the frontier a man made his own laws for those who wronged him.

No man could guess the thoughts of Ira Borden, and Bennett Kell did not try. He took a step aside, his eyes black with defiance. His hand clamped on his gun butt and he swallowed twice to get rid of the dryness in his throat.

"Outside of fighting in the war, I've never killed a man, Rickard," Bennett said tightly. "Unless you listen good and walk right, you'll be the first. We got two hundred of your cows. When we split up the money, my share was sixty dollars. Ever since I talked with you that day, I've had you on my mind. I figured when I got back to my ranch on the Brazos, I'd round up two hundred head of my own stock and drive them to you. I'll still do that, Rickard, or I'll pay you sixty dollars when I get it. But one thing sure, I won't let you hang me."

Nat Rickard's eyes remained hard and unblinking. "We'll see what Borden says."

"I say he stays with me. What he says makes it sound like he wants to make up for the mistakes he's made. When he acts otherwise, Rickard, you've got no cause to worry about me. I'll hang him myself!"

Impatience and annoyance still edged Borden's voice. He turned his back to Rickard, indicating his decision was made. He tilted his head toward Bennett, nodded with finality, and motioned for Bennett to follow him back to the camp.

His crew at his back, his gun in his hand, Borden

looked across the grass at Nat Rickard's unbelieving face and bawled an order at the man. "We'll stand here and watch while you get your men on their horses and turn back to Texas. Take my word for it, Rickard. Don't ride up on me again with a gun in your hand."

Rickard obeyed and Borden watched the Texans depart with anger still frosting his eyes. He did not mention the incident to Bennett again and he made no explanations to the curious crew. A moment later it seemed he had forgotten the whole episode. He glanced at the rising sun and said, "We've lost some time. The longer you stand here, the longer you'll ride after dark to make it up."

Ten

They reached the Red River in mid-afternoon, and there the Horseshoe lost its first man. Everything seemed normal when the cattle caught the scent of water, and movement in the herd quickened. A steer bellowed, another lifted its head. Horns clacked, hoofs churned and the drivers caught the signal.

"Hi-i-i-i-yi-i-i!" cried a voice from the flankers, and a horse snorted as eager spurs shot forward. It was a time to rest, a time to relax, a time to celebrate. Weary, sweating, slow-moving men detoured around the mass of moving bodies and hurried to take a look at the sluggish team.

But Ira Borden was already there. He'd been riding point for the past three days, his hat jammed hard on his bristling gray hair, his frost-gray eyes looking always northward. In a way, his interest had given Bennett encouragement, but in another it had worried him. It was good to know that the rancher's interest had been diverted from Bonnie Gray and was again centered on the progress of the drive. But Borden was like a madman, riding at point a while, checking the flanks, falling back to the drag and coming forward again. He was asking more of the men than human beings could give, and that was how they lost a man at the Red.

When they came to the river, Bennett was less than twenty feet from the rancher's side. He saw Borden's shaggy head lift to gaze northward, swing back over the herd, and look northward again. These gestures told him what was coming and his pulse quickened. Before he could utter a word of caution, Ira Borden wheeled his mount and glared at the riders who were crowding close.

Borden's eyes fastened on Monte Cole, and the wiry rider fingered his horse's reins uneasily. "Get back where you belong, Monte," Borden said. His voice was even, but the deep tones crackled with authority. "That goes for the rest of you. You've all seen a river before. Quit gawking at it and let's put these cattle across!"

With a swing of a lass rope, Borden lashed a lead steer into the water. He followed it, forcing another steer with him, and his bellowing voice dared the herd to defy him. No glance at the men he commanded, no time for discussion or argument. Ira Borden had spoken, and he expected no questions.

"Hold it, Borden," Bennett Kell called sharply. He swung his horse around, pushed it into the stream beside the stolid rancher. His black eyes met the man's cold gaze. "You said we'd came here in three days. We're here. The men are ready to drop, so let's camp. We can cross in the morning."

Ira Borden's chin fell to his chest. His shaggy brows

drew close to his frosty eyes and his thin lips tightened against his teeth.

"Kell," he said, "we hit it lucky here, coming right in to a shallow spot like this. Look at the sky up there. Take a look at the sky, and try to act like a ramrod instead of a nursemaid. I'm not concerned about making these men like me. I'm concerned about getting these cows to Missouri."

Bennett had been so intent on the herd that he had paid no attention to the weather. But now, as he sat facing Borden, he was aware that he cast no shadow. From the tail of his eye, he could see thin gray clouds floating close to the distant horizon. This was a land which saw no rain for six months, and then rocked under a cloudburst overnight. It could happen now. Within the next few hours, the Red could be running deep and dangerous and no steer would wet a hoof in it.

Slowly, Bennett turned away, nodding. He said quietly. "Well, here's where we shake Texas dirt off our feet, Ira."

Borden's rope swung again. A steer ventured out six feet, splashed wildly and sought refuge at the edge of the herd. "Bring the critters in, Kell!" Borden shouted, and Bennett backed his horse from the water.

Half a dozen riders sat staring at him. A few paces in front, Farley Jones was standing afoot, his arm resting on the pommel of his saddle.

"You heard the man yell," Bennett said, forcing a grin. "Let's earn our wages."

"Not me," Farley Jones said. "I've had all I aim to take. This is as far as I go."

Some time before, Farley Jones had spoken to the

109

others. They knew his thoughts, knew his plans, and they were waiting to see him make his stand. They wanted to follow his move, but they were clinging precariously to something that Farley Jones had forsaken; they had their pride, and they waited to see how fate dealt with a man who surrendered it.

"There's no wages for you if you pull out now, Farley," Bennett said. "Have you thought about that?"

"So there's no wages. But at least I stay alive. Maybe that ain't important to you and Borden. But it's important to four little 'uns I left in Crosscut, and it's important to the missus. Nobody's goin' to look after them but me. I aim to turn my horse right here and go back to them. I don't aim to die for a man like Ira Borden. He don't care about nobody but hisself."

"Nobody's asking you to die," Bennett replied quietly. "We're asking you to live, to take something back to that family. We're asking you to help Texas get on its feet again."

Doubt showed in Farley Jones's eyes for a fleeting second. He sent a speculative glance across the river, held it there a long time, then shook his head soberly.

"I can't do it, Bennett. Once in my life I've been out of Texas. That's when I went to Shiloh to fight with the troops. Right here's where I stop. I don't aim to step outside of Texas again. I got a feeling I'll never come back when I do."

There was a quaver in the man's voice. He brushed at his eyes, tugged at his ragged campaign hat and jabbed a foot at a stirrup. In another moment, the tears would show and this was a sight Bennett Kell did not want to see.

He shrugged and wheeled his horse. Ira Borden was

110

waiting for him. The rancher had moved forward to survey the situation, and his face was wry with disapproval.

"You're going to let him have his way, Kell?"

"I can't stop him without killing him. Nobody can."

"That may be true," Borden grunted. "But I expect my foreman to hold a crew together. When Jones gets away easy another will follow . . . then another, and another. We'll be riding by ourselves, you and me." Borden lowered his voice to a thick whisper. "I want them to know a man can't turn his back on his job and still call himself a man."

Bennett acted without taking time to weigh his own feelings. A yank at the reins, a jab of the spurs, and he was out of the water. He drew rein beside Jones, fought the excited horse to a standstill, and dragged the man from the saddle.

Jones landed on his feet and waited. There was no change in the expression on his round, flat-featured face, no cry of anger or surprise.

"You're yellow to the bone," Bennett grunted, coming down beside him.

The goading words were as much for the benefit of Bennett Kell as for Farley Jones. It was a fight he did not want, and he tried to generate enough anger to make it seem genuine. He still went at the task with reluctance, but it was a fight which had to come. Ira Borden wanted it, and perhaps he deserved it, Bennett admitted. He should have challenged Jones without Borden's instruction.

Bennett cursed Jones, trying to draw the first blow. But the man only stood and stared at him. Bennett hit him, the back of his hand slapping viciously at Farley's mouth, popping like a whip's crack. Blood oozed from cracked lips, and the puncher started swinging with both arms.

Bennett stepped easily aside, feeling a sense of pity at the man's awkwardness. Grimacing, hating the job, he clubbed Farley's temple with a knotted fist. The man staggered and fell, hunting the ground with his hands. One quick step, and Bennett towered over him again. He lifted Farley by the shirt front, slammed a fist directly into the man's face, and dropped him to the ground like an empty feed sack.

"I—I'm no fighter," Farley Jones whimpered. He wiped blood from his nose and looked up at Bennett, his eyes pleading. "You can see that, Kell. All I want to do is—is go home."

Bennett's lips were tight and unyielding. He paused to get his breath, his brow furrowed by a deep scowl. Seeing the hesitation in him, Farley Jones shoved to his feet and ran drunkenly toward his horse.

He almost made it. Bennett waited until the man was reaching for the horn before he dived at Farley's legs. They went down in a tangle of arms and legs. The horse slobbered and shied away. A sobbing, retching sound rattled in Farley's throat. It sounded like the crying of a child, and Bennett closed his ears against it.

Now there was haste and determination in Bennett's every move. The fight had already lasted too long for his conscience. He wanted it to end so he could begin forgetting it.

Farley Jones no longer attempted to defend himself against the merciless power in Bennett's long arms and wide shoulders. Bennett's fists kept pounding at him, rocking the puncher from side to side, peeling off skin

112

and piling up lumpy blue bruises.

More than once he wanted to quit, but he kept at it to make sure there never would be cause for another beating like it. This had to be more than a whipping, more than mere physical pain to punish a man. He had to whimper and cower and crumble in a way which would shame all who watched him.

Finally, it was done. Jones fell on his face in the dirt, his arms wrapped around his head. His shoulders twitched and ragged sobs tore at his chest.

His fists beating the grass around him, Jones lay on his belly and begged Bennett not to hit him again. He begged for a chance to see his wife again, to hold his children on his knee, to look for a job that would keep him near them.

One of the Horseshoe riders cursed under his breath and turned away. He was followed by the others, all silent; all with frozen expressions of disgust on their faces.

Chest heaving, his face streaked with sweat and grime, Bennett followed them. He walked with his head down, his eyes dull and listless. His mind drifted back to the night he had left Missouri—the night Toby Rusk and Wally Bryan had beaten him because he was quitting the border gangs. This was what they had been trying to do to him.

As he swung into saddle, he heard the creak of harness and the rattle of spurs as a horse went swiftly away from the river. He kept his eyes straight ahead, not wanting a final look at Farley Jones. Instead, he faced north and raised his arm.

It was a signal the drovers understood. Voices rose in a shout, horses nickered and the cattle changed position. On Borden's schedule they had reached the Red and on Borden's schedule they would cross it.

In an hour the line was solid and the confusion was gone. A steer clambered up the far bank, and the others filled its tracks. They followed, one after another, kept close by the flankers, pushed on by the drag men, until a solid line of cattle bridged the river.

From a rise near the northern bank, Bennett sat his saddle and watched the last stragglers splash their way ashore. Instead of triumph, he knew a feeling of guilt, and occasionally his glance skipped over the broad land to the south.

Ben Lufton, satisfied with the safety of his remuda, saw him there and galloped up to rest beside him. He said, "Don't fret too much over what happened with Farley. That's the penalty for being a ramrod. Sometimes you have to do what's best for a whole outfit instead of what's fair to one. Farley had to eat a lot of crow, but it may help the Horseshoe get to Missouri."

"You think it's worth it, Ben?"

The wrangler shrugged. "I allow you can answer that better than me. You rode all the way to Texas just to prove something. It's making you a hard man—almost as hard as Ira Borden, maybe."

"And the worst is still to come," Bennett said solemnly. He fumbled in his shirt pocket for the cigar stub. A moment after it was alight, he turned and smiled thinly at the short, hawk-nosed old man at his side. "Remind me never to make a trail drive without you, Ben. You're a comfort to a man."

He lifted the reins to move on, but the wrangler stopped him with a questioning look. "That question we was kicking around a minute ago, Bennett . . . You

114

never did answer it. Is there more ahead of us than any of us can make pay out for our own good?"

"You knew what was ahead of you before you left the Trinity," Bennett said shortly, and nudged his horse.

But as he rode away his face was clouded with guilt. The lie had not come easily for Bennett, and he wondered how long he could deceive a man as observant as Ben Lufton.

Sooner or later, he thought, he would have to tell all of them about Toby Rusk and Wally Bryan.

Eleven

A gloomy sky pushed darkness close to the ground, and night came early on the Red. The cattle were bedded close to the river's edge, shuffling restlessly as lightning fingered the edges of the heavy gray clouds overhead.

Beside the fire, tired and silent men cast uneasy glances at the herd; cattle could spook easily on a night like this. Bert Roscoe, propped on his saddle two feet from Bennett's own, rolled his head aside and said, "At least they'll run north if they stampede. They ain't about to cross that river again."

"Let's pray they don't run anywhere, Bert." Bennett rose and started off toward the remuda. "Just the same I think I'll have a look."

He paused as Ira Borden stepped into the edge of the campfire's light. Always busy, the rancher had been with the cattle since supper. He looked past Bennett to the shadows beyond, to the spot where Wade Zumbro and Bonnie Gray sat staring absently into the fire.

116

"You can come off that wagon tomorrow, Zumbro," Borden said flatly. "We can use you from here on out." Without waiting for an answer, he walked away, picked up his slickered bedroll and stomped off in the darkness to sleep alone.

Wade Zumbro flexed the fingers of his left hand. He moved his sore shoulder experimentally and nodded grimly to himself. He had not spoken to Bennett since the night of the shooting. But often during the day, and sometimes at the night camp, Bennett found the man's eyes on him, studying him. And now, for a brief moment, Zumbro raised his gaze to stare at Bennett Kell. Instinctively, Bennett tensed, his hand hovering close to his gun. A hard smile touched Zumbro's lips. Then he dropped his glance, said good night to Bonnie and went toward his blankets.

As Bonnie started toward her own bed in the supply wagon, she crossed deliberately in front of Bennett. She forced him to meet her glance, and her soft almond eyes seemed to make a desperate effort to speak to him. A faint, almost timid smile touched her lips and her steps slowed as she neared him. Bennett stared stonily at her, his face hard and unrelenting. The girl went on then, her dark head lifting in its characteristic haughty pose, but Bennett could not put her completely out of his mind as he rode toward the restless herd. Perhaps the pressure of the drive was making him too hard and distrustful, he thought. There had been a message of some kind in Bonnie's eyes. What had the girl wanted to tell him?

He circled the herd twice and came back to the remuda feeling no better about the temper of the night.

Head down, his mind drugged with weariness, he was almost abreast of a clump of greasewood before he saw Bonnie standing in the deep shadow of it.

"I wanted to talk with you," she said quietly.

She stayed where she was, her hands clasped in front of her, until he walked over to stand facing her. The face turned toward him seemed incredibly young and innocent, and he felt that somehow there was about her a subdued tenderness that had not been hers two weeks ago.

"Why have you been giving me the dodge, Bennett?"

"I've had some cows to drive," he said dryly. "That's my job. Why are you concerned about me?"

The familiar fire shone briefly in her dark eyes. Then she stared at the ground. "I'm not concerned about you. I'm concerned about me. Since that—that night in the wagon you think I'm a bad girl. I don't want anybody to think that."

He breathed a weary sigh, waved his hand impatiently. "You tried to trade yourself for a sack of gold. Call it good or bad, it means trouble to me and I want no more of it. Now get back where you belong before somebody tries to make something of this."

A slender hand grabbed his arm as he started to turn away. Bonnie held on to him and forced him to face her again. "I tried to trick him," she said in a throaty whisper. "All I wanted was to get Wade's money and get out of this mess I got myself into. I'm tired of having everyone of you undressing me with your eyes every time I move, and I thought I could trick Borden into paying Wade. That's the way it was, Bennett. I explained it to Wade and he understood. You've got to understand it, too."

"All right," he said impatiently.

"You don't believe me. I'm a good girl, and I want you to know it. I'm not the kind you think I am."

"So?"

"So take me and see for yourself, Bennett. That way you'll know!" Before he could grasp the meaning of the girl's words, she threw herself into his arms and pressed her body hard against his. Her arms clung to his waist, long nails biting at the flesh of his back, and silent sobs shook her slender shoulders. "Take me, Bennett, and you'll be sorry you thought those things."

Far off in the distance thunder rumbled and rolled, but Bennett could not hear it for the pounding of his pulse. His arms closed about the slender girl, drawing her closer, and his head bent to kiss the soft bend of her neck where it joined the rounded flesh of her shoulder. Then as his lips brushed her flesh, the voice of sanity shouted him back to reality. He straightened, angry at himself, at Bonnie, at all the temptations which had hampered his journey. Rope-hardened hands tore at the girl's arms, pulling them free and shoving her roughly aside.

He stood staring at her shocked face, his breathing coming in gasps. "Get some sense in your head, Bonnie. Don't waste yourself trying to make the world sorry for doing you wrong. That's how I got here. If you're a decent woman don't mess things up by going wrong to prove a point. Now go back to camp. I'll wait a while."

She gave him a long, searching look, ending it with a sheepish smile. Behind her, the brush rustled faintly and alarm spread over her face. Signaling for silence, Bennett ducked low and sprinted forward, his glance sweeping the darkness ahead. He straightened, and called back to the girl, telling her it was safe for her to return to the wagon.

He gave her time to reach the camp and then went on himself. He walked with his hand on his gun and his stomach knotted with dread. He was certain that trouble waited somewhere ahead. Before he stopped running, Bennett had seen the silhouette of a man disappear behind another brush clump nearer the camp. Someone had been watching when Bonnie intercepted him. Someone had heard all that passed between them.

Briefly, Bennett debated the route he should take to the camp, then he shrugged, feeling this was not a situation he could evade, and walked directly toward the brush clump.

When he was five yards away, Wade Zumbro stepped into the open. Bennett stopped in his tracks. He spread his feet on the grass, settled his shoulders and let the fingers of his right hand dangle near the butt of his gun.

"I'm not calling for your gun, Kell," Zumbro said. "I wanted to shake your hand."

Bennett's eyes widened in surprise, and Zumbro moved up to stand an arm's length away. The man was smiling, and he spoke in calm, even tones.

"I was spying on Bonnie tonight," he said guiltily. "But I won't do that again. I learned something about her and I learned something about you. You're more of a man than I've met before. You'll get no more aggravation from me."

The smile went off Zumbro's face, but he kept his glance level. At last Bennett held out his hand, and Zumbro grasped it firmly.

120

"I'll sleep real sound tonight for the first time, Kell."

"I wouldn't advise that for anybody," Bennett said. "Tonight the cattle may run. Tomorrow the border gangs may send out their scouts."

At dawn the rain came in a steady drizzle but the cattle ducked their heads and moved off the bed grounds without incident. Ira Borden guided his horse in and out among the bobbing horns, lining up the leaders, stretching them out on the trail. His booming voice barked orders at the flankers and cursed the stragglers and quitters among the cattle. Close beside him, Wade Zumbro worked silently and with seeming unconcern. He favored his left shoulder slightly, but he kept a lass rope swinging and guided his horse with pressure from his knees.

Ahead of the herd, picking a trail, Bennett paused to let the others catch up. He hooked a leg over the horn, twisted to look back at the moving cattle. But his mind stayed on them only a moment. Without realizing it, he let his glance drift back toward the Red and to the vast land that lay beyond.

He was still sitting that way when Cass Bailey's chuck wagon rumbled close. Cass said, "I reckon you're fretting some about Farley Jones out there."

"I'd feel better if he had some food, Cass. A man can live off the land, but it's hard."

"He's got food," Cass grunted. "I packed his saddle bags full an hour before the fight started. A man gets a hunch about some things."

Bennett smiled, knowing he would not worry any

more about Jones, and dropped back to ride with the others.

From the drifters of the past, from the tales they had heard and the sign they could read, the men of the Horseshoe knew where the trail lay now. Across a corner of The Nations, where you could meet a Comanche or Kiowa or Osage with paint on his face and death in his eyes. North and eastward at first, picking up traces of the old Sedalia Trail where other men had tried to reach the railroad, and then north again toward Arkansas and Missouri.

They paced it off a mile at a time, a day at a time, and tensions eased. Around the night fires there was laughter and teasing and boasting again. Gradually Bonnie became a part of the great adventure and the men began to accept her as a member of the crew.

She was no longer the haughty, arrogant girl who had defended her weakness by flaunting her charms before the Horseshoe crew. Almost overnight her manner had changed. Bennett had sensed the difference on the morning following her hysterical appeal for respect, when she had challenged him to test her virtue. That day she had risen at dawn, surprising Cass Bailey with her eagerness to help him cook breakfast. She had been Cass's assistant ever since, lending a special touch to the plain food of a trail hand's meal.

In the evenings Bonnie brought out needle and thread and spent her time repairing the threadbare garments with which Ira Borden had stocked the supply wagon. She accepted the crew's compliments and praise with the grace of a mature woman. And when she smiled her gratitude the men read nothing

122

more into the gesture than was meant.

Luck rode with the Horseshoe and spirits were high until the day they sighted the bones. It was a startling sight, frightening to a man who saw it for the first time. The bones were strewn for a mile across the floor of a shallow valley, more than a hundred dry, disjointed skeletons. Horned skulls, arched ribs and smaller shanks glistened grotesquely in the evening sun.

Ira Borden, riding far back the line, put his horse into a gallop to overtake Bennett. The rancher brought his mount to a sliding halt, stepped to the ground and kicked at a heap of bones. He swung his bleak gaze around the brush-covered hills, and motioned for Bennett to dismount.

"I don't like this, Kell," Borden growled. He settled his hands on his hips, stared speculatively at Bennett's perspiring face. "Somebody slaughtered a herd here. I won't have my cows broken to pieces and laid out in the sun to rot."

"It won't happen to us, Ira. This was the Triangle D outfit out of Texas. It happened nearly a year ago, and word got around. Nobody has tried this trail since, and the gangs pulled away from this valley. That's why we're here. You've got to depend on what I know, Ira."

Ira Borden drew a deep breath. His fists clenched and relaxed indecisively and he frowned again at the scattering of bones. Through thinning lips he said, "We won't take a chance. We'll swing around and go back the way we came in. I don't like the looks of this place a little bit."

Borden's square back turned toward Bennett. His voice boomed in a loud "Ho-o-o!" to draw the attention of Wade Zumbro, who was pushing the leaders past the dismounted men.

Zumbro reined around and cocked his head to catch the rancher's words. At a wave from Borden, Zumbro trotted his horse closer, nodding as Borden yelled, "Swing fast and push hard at their heels, Zumbro. We're getting out of here and heading for the open country again. Tell the others!"

"Keep them coming as they are, Zumbro." Bennett strode forward to stand at Borden's shoulder. His dark eyes had a brooding look and his flat-planed face was ridged with muscle. "We bed down right here."

Zumbro jumped as though stung by a whip. A puzzled frown drew his brows together momentarily, then he grinned slyly. He relaxed, holding the reins loosely in his fingers. Zumbro had faced Borden's wrath, and he knew the sting of it. Now he was only a bystander and he settled down to enjoy the clash that was sure to come.

Ira Borden's breath made a hissing sound. A vein throbbed in his temple, and his boots scuffed up dust as he wheeled to look at Bennett Kell.

"You're getting too big for your britches, Kell. Don't run off at the mouth when I'm talking."

Sudden fury shook Bennett's tall frame and put a curt edge in his voice. He said, "Then don't talk so damn much, Ira. You can stop giving the orders you hired me to give. You're paying me to take this herd to Missouri. I can't do it if you keep driving the men like mules and keep acting like you know more about this country than I do. Let's get it straight, Ira. I boss this drive from now on."

Ira Borden took a single step forward. His frost-gray eyes glistened like ice against his leathery skin. His broad chest rose and fell, and he let the silence run on until it grated against Bennett's nerves. And then Borden's jaws puffed slightly as his tongue rolled against his cheek. His lips tightened, and he inhaled noisily.

"You ever spit on me, mister," Bennett Kell said sharply, "and I'll shoot you like a dog."

Twelve

Gunfire and death were born of such beginnings. Bennett knew it and every nerve in his body was vibrant with that awareness. Ira Borden knew it too, and suddenly he seemed incredibly calm. Borden would consider the worth of such a risk, things to be lost or gained.

A principle hung in the balance, and strength would be measured during the time it took for one to lose his temper—or his nerve. Sweat glistened on Bennett Kell's forehead and trickled into his eyes and he thought of the failure which would mark his life if he died here. He thought, too, of Farley Jones lying in the dust sobbing, and he gritted his teeth against the urge to grab for his gun. And he listened at the same time to an inner voice which kept asking: *Can I beat him?*

He knew when the moment of decision came. Ira Borden drew himself up tall, set his hands on his hips. The rawboned old man swayed forward a trifle, as though to look deeper into Bennett's eyes.

"I think you'd do it," Borden said. "I think you'd kill me, but I'm not sure I know the reason."

"To get these cows to Missouri, maybe. But mostly to keep this crew alive."

A faint nod of the grizzled head, a casual shifting of booted feet and Borden was through with the situation. He swung aboard his horse and said to Zumbro, "You heard what your ramrod said. Bring them in and bed them down."

That was all. Borden made no apologies and no explanations. He spoke with action and Zumbro understood. Borden had met a will as strong as his own, a man too hard and determined to be bossed and badgered and maneuvered like a puppet.

"Word gets around, somebody might build a statue of you in Texas, Kell," Zumbro grinned as Bennett took his place with the cattle.

Bennett chuckled, but he did not feel triumphant. All around him were the signs of another's hopes and another's failure. Here the Triangle D outfit had been crushed and killed, and the skeletons were only a few of the thousands which dotted the various trails that had kept pace with the railroad's progress westward. Bennett had heard the story from Toby Rusk and he knew it could be believed. Rusk had been riding with the gang which stampeded the Triangle D and Rusk had told him that the gangs no longer watched for a herd to come this way.

But things could have changed since Bennett left Missouri. Perhaps even Toby Rusk would outguess him and pick this spot to attack. He consoled himself with the hope that it was too far south for Rusk to ride but he continued to be plagued by uneasiness. If Rusk was not here there could easily be others like him.

Throughout the night Bennett made a show of confidence. The others watched his face, studied his movements, and he spent more time with the crew than usual. He kept them busy with trivial talk of cattle breeding, bronc riding and the subjects cowboys know best. Gradually he saw the glances toward the scattered bones subside, and the Horseshoe crew began to relax.

All through the next day the scene was much the same but Bennett was no longer concerned about hiding his feelings. Cattle bones lined the trail at regular intervals, and Bennett had no promise of safety to fulfill this night. Rearing against the northern horizon were bare brown bluffs, standing silent and stark against the timbered ridges of Missouri. This was what the men of Texas called the Boneyard Trail and the Horseshoe crew knew where they rode, knew the danger that hovered near.

Not a man spoke of his fears when the camp was made. As Ira Borden came in for his supper, he stopped first at the supply wagon. When he joined the crew he carried an assortment of cartridge boxes in his arms. He set them down on the trampled ground and, without speaking, filled his plate and began to eat. One at a time the men visited the spot. New brass shells gleamed in every loop of their gunbelts. Later there was the sound of pistol cylinders clicking and turning while the drovers cleaned their guns.

As the yellow twilight faded to darkness, Borden turned a quizzical gaze toward Bennett Kell. He said, "We're in the hunting grounds of the border raiders now. In broad daylight we might see them coming. But there's a lot of us here. At night they could ride in on us while we sat here thinking it was one of our own. Have you thought about that Kell?"

Nodding, Bennett rose and moved out into the circle of light. His dark face was taut, his voice solemn with concern. "If we're smarter than they are, and tougher than they are, we'll get past them. But we'll have to watch every bush, every draw and stand of trees from here to the railhead. We've had a lot of luck but don't count on any more of it. Don't expect to see Kansas City without a fight. It ain't going to happen."

Wade Zumbro, lying on an elbow directly in front of him, twisted around and sat erect. He said, "You promised to take us through. You gave Ira your word."

"I remember that. You'll get through if you listen to me and fight hard enough when the time comes."

"You seem pretty sure about that fight. How come?"

Almost it was as though Bennett Kell was back on the Trinity. The weeks since he first rode up to Ira Borden's roundup seemed like years, but the knot in his stomach was the same. It was the same as when he looked Borden in the eye and admitted that he'd ridden with a border gang. But he had driven himself deliberately to this point. Just as he had felt compelled to throw the last of his outlaw wages in the dirt at Toby Rusk's feet, he could not evade the fair and honest course now. It had been pestering his mind since the day they crossed the Red.

"You seem dead certain we'll get it," Zumbro murmured again.

"It was promised to me," Bennett said quietly. "The

129

men I rode with didn't like it when I pulled out. They warned me not to come back."

Ira Borden came to his feet with the ease of a young buck. He took a step forward, squared his shoulders. "Does this trail lead toward the camp you bossed up here?"

Both suspicion and wavering trust were in Borden's tone. Bennett felt a quick rise of anger but he forced himself to remain calm. Borden had a right to ask the question.

"We'll miss my outfit by twenty miles, Borden. But it doesn't matter. Men like Toby Rusk and Wally Bryan will find us. They've got to steal for a living and they've got to make sure a man like me can't turn his back on them and change sides. If they don't the rest of the gang will drift off one at a time and they'll be out of business."

Borden sank to the ground, apparently satisfied. Bennett studied the faces of the others a moment, looking for accusation or distrust in their eyes. He saw none, and he breathed a silent sigh. His nerves were suddenly at ease. A man's past was of little concern to those who had known no part of it. The Horseshoe crew measured Bennett Kell by the standards of a turbulent land, and they had not found him lacking. A question had been asked, the answer given, and now they awaited their orders.

He said, "We'll double the nighthawks. Hereafter no man wears a hat after dark. You won't get sunburned without it, so hitch it to your blankets as soon—"

"Now lookee here," Scrap Dooley objected. "I feel plumb naked without—"

"Shoot anything you see wearing a hat," Bennett cut in sharply. "That's how we'll tell friend from foe."

The order stood and there was no need to repeat it. As they moved on into the round-toped knolls of Missouri, it became custom for the men to bare their heads at sundown. But the Horseshoe's luck held, and there was no hint of violence from any quarter. Bennett's face became drawn and his movements grew jumpy. The peace and tranquility became an annoying, torturing existence, and he found himself wishing that his searching glance could pick up some suspicious sign. It could not go on this way, and the waiting was fraying the nerves of everyone.

Sleep was almost a forgotten thing for Bennett. He sought the refuge of his blankets only when exhaustion pulled him down. Then he was up in an hour, circling wide around the herd, inspecting every brush clump, whispering warnings to the nodding nighthawks.

It was on one of these midnight forays that Bennett spotted the first hat. He was riding the faithful dun, feeling the need for luck, and his course lay across a mile-long swale which divided the bowl-shaped hollow in which they were camped. Chokecherry bushes and red cedar sprouts filled the long depression, and Bennett could not rest until he was sure it was deserted.

Keeping the horse at a walk, he started across the nearest tip of the sink, meaning to begin at the rear and circle back across the front of it. He was into the brush, ducking his head to slide under a spindly oak, when the dun nickered softly. Quickly, Bennett swung his head from side to side. Then he saw the movement off to the left. First a shadow, then a bobbing head. But the sight

131

that stirred his blood and sent shivers along his spine was the peaked crown of a cowman's hat.

His first impulse was to grab for the rifle in the saddle boot beneath his knee, to follow the orders he had issued to the others. But the experience of the past few days had made him impatient and angry. He was tired of waiting, tired of not knowing what lay ahead and how many eyes were watching them. A shot in the dark might kill an advance scout, but it would leave perhaps a score of others unscathed. And a sudden blast of gunfire could stampede the herd, start cattle running over men and wagons and a hundred miles of strange land.

Keen black eyes still on the man's hiding place, Bennett slid silently from his horse, letting the reins drop to the ground. He went off on the balls of his feet, telling himself: *Here's where we find out who we're fighting!*

Ahead of him the brush rustled. A shadow darted deeper into the sink, silhouetted momentarily against the pale blue of a moonlit sky. The scout had heard him coming, and secrecy was now abandoned. As Bennett quickened his pace, the man broke into a run. Somewhere ahead, Bennett heard a horse stamp restlessly and he shifted his course in that direction.

There they met, coming into the open on opposite sides of the horse. Head ducked low, shaggy black hair streaming across his eyes, Bennett sprinted for the long-legged sorrel. Beneath the horse, he could see legs pumping toward him, and he left his feet in a hurtling dive.

Under the horse Bennett went, belly-down and

stirring up grass and dirt. The horse skittered away, and Bennett grabbed at a man's tottering leg. At the same instant, he rolled away, searching desperately for the butt of his gun.

A moment of fear and panic touched him then. His hand scraped an empty holster. The Colt had slipped out when he fell. Beside him a shadowy shape was scrambling to a sitting position. Starlight flashed on blued steel, and Bennett knew the man had a gun in his hand and was trying to get it in firing position.

Bennett lashed out with his boot. He felt the hard contact of metal sting his instep, and the raider grunted as the boot grazed his chin. The gun made a solid thump as it landed on the ground somewhere farther on.

The scout showed no inclination for a rough-and-tumble brawl. He wanted his gun. Shoving to his feet, the man went in a staggering run toward the spot where the weapon had landed.

Bennett started to follow, but the edge of his glance saw his own .45 lying less than a yard away. He threw himself forward, grabbing the weapon and cocking it while he rested on his elbows.

A man with ears tuned to danger knows the sound of a gun hammer's click. Like a man caught in a rope, the border raider halted, his shoulders squeezing together fearfully as he raised his hands.

"Don't shoot," he cried, and his voice had the fear of death in it.

"You start backing up here like a crawfish then." Bennett got to his feet, his breath coming in hard gasps. He waited until the man's back came within his reach, then stopped him with a nudge of the gun barrel.

"I—I was just passin' through," the man said. "I don't want no trouble."

Bennett jerked at the man's shoulder, whirled him around to look at his face. He'd seen a hundred like it. A bitter, unfeeling face with a savage twist to the thin lips and a coldness in the pale blue eyes. A man with the hide vest and rolled levis of a working cowman, but a man with the sallow skin of those who rode mostly at night and spent their leisure under oil lamps.

"You got more trouble than a steer with hook-worms," Bennett said. "I know who you are and why you're here. But I want to know more. I want to know where the rest of the gang is and I want to talk with the boss."

A flicker of surprise showed in the man's pale eyes. Then the cold stare returned. He said, "I'm riding south, looking for a riding job. Nobody in these parts knows me, I know nobody. You might as well let me go, friend."

For a moment Bennett stared into the sharp-boned face, reading the unshaken resolve now that the man had a chance to talk his way out. Bennett's mouth tightened and he balanced himself on one foot, suddenly inspired by the throbbing ache which strenuous activity continued to send through his shoulder. A puzzled frown creased the raider's face, but a jab of Bennett's gun distracted his curious glance.

When he planted both feet solidly on the ground again, Bennett's left hand held a sharp-roweled spur. He reached forward, raked the star wheel lightly across the scout's cheek. The man drew away with a curse. His

134

hand lowered tentatively toward his face, hesitated, and lifted above his shoulder again.

"What was that for?"

"Just a sample," Bennett grunted. "I'm going to stand here with this gun in your belly and this spur in my hand. If you try to move, I'll kill you. But every time I ask you a question, I expect an answer. When I don't get one, I aim to use this spur on your face. I'll cut you up like rawhide unless you talk, mister."

The man's pale eyes searched Bennett's face. What he saw made his chin quiver slightly and brought a resigned sigh from his lips.

"All right," he said, swallowing hard. "I ride with the Nelse Garwood gang. Nelse will maybe understand how you could put a gun on me and make me bring you in. But he ain't ever going to overlook a man who runs off at the mouth. Keep that gun on me, and we'll ride into the hills. But that's all the talking you're going to hear from me, friend."

Bennett nodded. He refused to consider the fool-hardiness of his mission, but he knew the scout's agreement suited his purpose. It would be of no benefit to know about Garwood's strength and location if the herd was to be attacked, anyway. What he had to do was stop the fight before it started.

With the scout's own rope, Bennett tied the man to the saddle and led the sorrel through the brush to his own horse. Afterward, they rode toward the ragged line of hills which hemmed the Horseshoe herd in from the east, the cowed raider showing the way willingly.

Only once was the silence of the trip broken. At the mouth of a gushing creek, the raider turned and gave

Bennett a curious stare. He said, "You ain't very smart, friend. You've figured out a way to get in to see Nelse Garwood but you ain't figured a way out. We'll likely bury you at sunup."

"That's a gamble I'll have to take."

The raider frowned thoughtfully. "Or maybe you figure to join up with Nelse and split the profit on that herd."

"Maybe," Bennett grunted impatiently, and tipped the barrel of his gun as a signal for the man to keep moving.

Thirteen

Five miles along the gushing creek a sandstone bluff jutted across the bare-topped hills. Flashing against its dark bulk were a dozen scattered fires. The hum of voices echoed in the night.

His first look at the border gang's camp sent a stab of apprehension through Bennett Kell. It aroused another emotion in him, a feeling hard to identify, like a mixture of pity and disdain.

These were the voices of Missouri in a strange and confused era, he thought. Bold and defiant voices of men who posted no lookouts for protection and hid in the hills only for the benefit of suprising their victims during an attack. They were not hunted men, as an outlaw is hunted, and no lawman held a specific charge against them.

They rode for a cause, defended a right, and the law was far removed from them. This was the excuse for their outlawry and at the beginning there was sincerity and purpose behind it. The Texans caused them trouble. The first herds headed for far-off Illinois had

137

crossed this land as far back as 1860, and they had left disease in their wake. On the Missouri farms milk cows dropped dead and foundation stock was wiped out. The farmers found a name for it. Texas fever, they called it, and Texans were warned to stay away. After the war, the situation got worse. Kansans came across the line and brought their guns. Kansans who held no sympathy for the South's stand and still wanted to fight.

Texas fever became a crutch to stand on, a cause to rally around, and the cutthroats made the most of it. They used it to settle a war-born grudge or to fill their pockets with cash. And who could blame a man for defending his rights?

Bennett Kell could blame them. He had used the same crutch, and he rode into the raiders' camp with hate strengthening his nerve. He had watched the work of such men; watched Toby Rusk and his own gang make a mockery of a cause; watched them gloat over their spoils; watched the blood-lust grow.

But what could a lone man do against them? Bennett did not yet know, but he felt that an effort had to be made. Big Jim McKittridge had asked him to whip the border gangs, to push a Texas herd past them so the railroad would have a reason for building. Bennett's reward would be self-respect and McKittridge's blessing when he married Ada.

To Bennett the reward was big enough. It was his only escape from the border gangs, from a life that had grown out of a desire for revenge, only to sicken him when he found the deep principles bred within him rebelled against it.

Now he was among them again, riding to meet a man

whose name was whispered in camps such as these all along the trail. Bennett's mind sorted over the stories he had heard of Nelse Garwood and for the first time his determination wavered. His gun was still lined on his captive's back but his mind was struggling with indecision.

The man in front of him made a turn to the left, going toward the end of the bluff. Bennett swerved his horse to follow, but he told himself: "I ought to swing my horse around and run like hell."

A moment later he pushed the thought aside, his attention going to a crude log shack which loomed suddenly in front of them. "We're here," the captured raider said and dismounted with the awkwardness forced upon a man whose hands are bound at his back.

A man moved out from the shadow of the doorway, asking, "Who've you got with you, Matt?"

Bennett answered the question, eager to press his luck all at once and learn the outcome of his daring mission. He dismounted, still holding the gun, and stepped close enough to see the man in front of the shack.

"Bennett Kell," he said. He spoke calmly, but he felt the coldness of fear in his stomach. "I put a gun on your man and made him bring me here."

"That's right, Nelse," the pale-faced rider put in hurriedly. "He caught me unawares and I didn't have a chance."

Nelse Garwood chuckled dryly. "You can go get somebody to untie your hands and turn in." As the man started away, Garwood called: "And, Matt . . . you can quit telling us how tough you are now."

He chuckled again, his eyes following Matt's sheepish retreat, and it seemed he had forgotten Bennett Kell's presence. After a moment he backed toward the cabin, adjusted a flat rock which was propped beside the doorway, and sat down with a sigh.

"Why don't you put that gun away, Kell, and have a seat?"

Bennett stared dubiously at him, still somewhat stunned by the man's manner and appearance. Nelse Garwood would have looked at home behind the teller's window of a bank. His hair was dark and thick, with a tinge of gray at the temples, and it looked as if he had just visited a barber. A neat man, a handsome, clean-cut man in his early forties who wore a Prince Albert coat and a string tie amid the brush and dust of a border gang's camp.

"Maybe I better stay right here a minute," Bennett said firmly. "I'm with that herd your man was scouting. I don't aim to have it cut up by your butchers."

Nelse Garwood gave him a sharp look. Now the clear blue eyes which had sparkled with amusement earlier held a hard glint.

"I've got fifty men scattered up and down this creek. I can put my fingers in my mouth and whistle and they will convene right here. Does that change your opinion?"

"Not much." The number of campfires had given him an idea of the gang's strength, and Bennett knew the Horseshoe was no match for them. "I measure strength by guts, not by numbers," he added bluntly.

Then he holstered his gun, squatted on his heels, fished for a cigar stub, and struck a match with his thumb. Through the smoke he raised his glance to see if his actions had the desired effect.

A smile touched Nelse Garwood's wide mouth. He chuckled and ran a soft hand across his bare head. "Perhaps we should quit sparring and get down to cases. Frankly, I'm curious about you. I recognized the name at once, of course, and I know who you are. The last time one of my men talked with Toby Rusk you fellows were picking up the crumbs just outside of Kansas City. Now what are you doing with a herd of Texas cattle?"

Bennett scowled, hiding the surprise he felt at Garwood's knowledge of his past. But did Garwood know it was his *past?* He puffed again on the cigar while he sought for the right words.

"Went after them," he said at last. "That seems one sure way of making a profit."

"Then you don't worry about Texas Fever?"

There was a note of derision in Garwood's voice, and Bennett felt a strange sense of revulsion at the question. He said, "Do you?"

Garwood shrugged. "Once I did. That's how I came to be here instead of in Kansas City practicing law. When I first came out to this country, I was impressed by the ignorance and futility of a great number of helpless people. I thought they needed a leader."

A wry smile twisted Garwood's lips, and his face turned solemn and thoughtful. At one of the fires a short distance away, a droning voice carried over the sound of others and Bennett strained his ears in unbelief. Someone was reading a Bible aloud. Garwood's glance caught him listening.

"You hear old man Taliafero," Garwood murmured. "He's still fighting for a cause. But he's the only one. The others want money—and blood."

141

"Not from my herd, Garwood. I brought them all the way from Texas, and I aim to load them in Kansas City."

"You stole that herd?"

Bennett's reaction was automatic. A month ago he might have grinned blandly, but now he did not like to be called a thief. His lips clamped tight and he eased to his feet, a thumb hooked in his gunbelt.

"I've got them," he said flatly.

Nelse Garwood rose, too. Calm, relaxed, a man whose face showed no strains or emotions. He brushed at a speck on his coat and smiled.

"You're the kind I need in this organization," Garwood said. "You don't have to tell a man you're hard as rock and tough as rawhide. It shows through after a while. That cattle outfit you've collected would probably put up the worst fight we've seen."

"So?"

"So we'll make a bargain. Cut out half the herd and leave it standing. You move on at daylight and we'll pick up our share. No one can get hurt that way."

Bennett shook his head. "It won't work, Garwood. You know Toby Rusk and Wally Bryan. Mister, I'm driving this herd right straight toward them. When they find out you've waylaid us, nothing but blood will satisfy them either. It's all right to steal from Texans, maybe, but when the gangs steal from each other you've got a private war on your hands. If you start it there'll be hell to pay all over Missouri."

It was a possibility Garwood could picture in his mind. He picked at his thumbnail thoughtfully. "I should take the chance, Kell. Some of my men are at the edge of poverty, and they won't get many more

142

chances at easy money. Neither will I. A few months from now I'll have to find my books again and look for a place to hang up my shingle. Our days here are running out. When the railroad gets out of our reach, this business will come to an end. Maybe it's the best thing."

"Then you won't cause me any trouble?"

Garwood studied Bennett's face. "That wasn't what I meant. My judgment tells me we ought to bring your case to court, let the men decide for themselves."

Alarm tightened Bennett's nerves, but he could afford to remain patient as long as Nelse Garwood's face reflected doubt. The men at the fires would be guided by greed and revenge, but surprisingly, Bennett had observed more human qualities in Nelse Garwood. As Bennett himself had been for so long, Nelse Garwood was at the brink of decision and there was evidence that he, too, had battled with his conscience. It was a straw in Bennett's favor, and he waited for it to show its weight.

"One thing disturbs me about you," Garwood frowned. "There's a lot of Texas in your talk. You say you're Bennett Kell, and I've accepted that. But my training tells me to ask for proof. I have no intention of being deceived by a smooth-talking Texan."

So far it had been too easy, and Bennett told himself he should have expected a challenge. But Garwood was asking proof that few men could provide. Bennett felt his hopes wane. For a man like Nelse Garwood, a letter with a name on it, an engraved watch, or initials on a hatband would not be enough. These things could be stolen, and Bennett was among thieves.

In Nelse Garwood's mind there would be an obvious

solution. He knew Toby Rusk and Wally Bryan. If Bennett would bring them here, Garwood would take their word. But, he knew, Toby Rusk and Wally Bryan would come here with him only one way—if they brought him dead.

"You're asking a whole lot," Bennett told him. "You say you're Garwood, but I'll lay you four to one you can't prove it."

"I don't have to. You do. Either that, or we'll select a jury from the men and hear your case. We may just have to risk that private war."

War! The single word made relief sweep through him. He slipped a hand into his boot top and withdrew a small oilskin folder. Slowly, he unwrapped it and brought out a creased and soiled document, which he held out for Garwood to read.

"My army discharge," Bennett said quietly. "You'll notice I was on the wrong side for Texas. They don't take too kindly to me, to tell the truth."

His face unchanging, Garwood read the name and inscription. He said solemnly, "There was no right side, Kell. You can ride out, now. I'd advise you to ride fast. I seldom change my mind, but this time it could happen."

"What about the men? How can I be sure?"

Garwood's face showed a tinge of red. "You can be sure because I'm their leader. I said your cattle are free to pass."

Their eyes met for a moment, and it seemed there was need for other words between them. At least a handshake, Bennett thought, but Nelse Garwood was already backing toward the flat rock, taking his seat again.

144

The dun lifted its head as though sensing victory. Without a backward look, Bennett mounted and headed down the creek bank. He realized for the first time that his shirt was plastered to his body with cold sweat, and that a terrible tiredness had come from his meeting with Nelse Garwood.

Still he was not completely at ease. The Horseshoe herd was only five miles away, guarded by a handful of weary men. And here behind these knolls were fifty experienced fighters. He wondered if the calm and immaculate Nelse Garwood was as much of a leader as he boasted, if he could hold them here while they knew a Texas herd walked almost within sight. . . .

He did not get a chance to ponder the question. A shot boomed behind him, and a slug whistled over his head. He kicked free of the stirrups and dived for the ground, his hand dragging out his own gun while he was in mid-air.

He landed with a breath-jarring jolt, looked wildly about for cover, and crawled swiftly behind a scrubby cedar. Up the creek he heard voices shouting excitedly. Hoofbeats sounded against the earth, and a rider came rapidly toward him.

Bennett Kell turned toward the sound. Garwood had played him for a fool and he'd fallen right into the trap.

Fourteen

While Bennett waited behind the cedar, the approaching horseman slowed momentarily at a turn in the trail. Then he came on at the pace of a man reading sign. Bennett eased the hammer back on his gun, his eyes fastened on the trail. He became aware of the dead cigar stub still clamped between his teeth, turned and spat it over his shoulder. It was the last of the cigars he had brought down the trail with him.

When he looked back at the path along the creek, Nelse Garwood was pulling a prancing bay to a halt twenty yards away. The gang leader's head swung from side to side. His glance settled on Bennett's dun which had trotted downstream a few feet and stopped.

Garwood cupped his hands around his mouth. "You all right, Kell?" he called.

"Fine," Bennett replied dryly. "I've got a bead on your belly. If you move I'll kill you."

Nelse Garwood appeared to relax. He placed his hands on the pommel and remained silent a moment.

At last he said, "Kell, that shot was fired against my orders. It was Matt Raymond, the scout you captured. He couldn't take the ribbing his cronies were giving him, so he had to prove how tough he is. Now we know he can't shoot straight either, so I don't guess we'll keep him with us much longer. Sorry, Kell. Good luck!"

The explanation had come in casual tones. But the stiffness of Garwood's bearing hinted at subdued anger. With his final words, Garwood turned his horse and went back toward the bluff.

For several minutes, Bennett stayed where he was, his ears cocked for sound. From the border gang's camp he could hear the hum of voices and the tread of moving feet, but no other rider tried to follow him. Still he held to his gun. And when he mounted the dun, he put the horse into a fast gallop, eager to put as much space as possible between him and the border gang.

Luke Ashley was standing guard with the remuda. He spotted the rider coming into the Horseshoe camp, weaving wearily in the saddle. Luke raised his rifle, his finger curling on the trigger. Then he saw Kell's bare head and he lowered the gun. He walked out a few paces to take the dun's reins, noticing the lather on the horse's flanks.

"You've had a hard ride, Bennett," Luke said.

"Enough for tonight. If you'll rub my horse a bit, I reckon I'll turn in."

There was curiosity in Ashley's sharp glance, perhaps suspicion. But Bennett was in no mood to explain. Fatigue dragged at him, and the strain of the night had left his brain numb and foggy. Now all he needed was rest. He was beginning to feel a small measure of contentment. Another obstacle had been met and overcome and he was a step nearer the goal he had set for himself.

With good fortune he would be in Kansas City in less than a week and there Ada McKittridge waited for him. She became more desirable in his memory with each passing day, and the long separation had deepened his love. But, after nearly two months' absence, he could no longer be sure of Ada's feelings. He wondered if she could be as eager and impatient for their reunion as he was.

Reluctantly he pushed the thought of her aside as he went quietly through the sleeping camp and unrolled his own bedroll. He could learn of Ada's faithfulness in only one way, he told himself as he sank to the ground. That was to fulfill his pledge to her uncle and hurry back to her.

Before he could get his boots off, Ira Borden walked out of the shadows near the chuck wagon and stopped beside him. The rancher took out his big brass watch, squinted at it, and returned it to his vest pocket.

"It's three o'clock in the morning, Kell." Borden tried to keep his voice low, but the hard bite of impatience was in it. "You've been gone since before midnight. I was getting concerned about you."

Borden's eyes said other things. He wanted to know where Bennett had been, and he meant to get an answer before he slept.

Bennett considered stalling Borden off with vague answers, but a look at the man's determined face told him such an approach would merely prolong the discussion. He said, "I've been doing some missionary work, Ira. We've had a border gang looking down our neck tonight. I nabbed their scout and made him take me to the boss. I persuaded them to lay off the Horseshoe."

He told Borden the whole story of his visit to Nelse Garwood's camp, wanting to end the matter and go to sleep. When he had finished, he yanked his boots off and fell back on his blankets with an exhausted sigh.

Borden stood where he was, a gaunt, statue-like shadow in the gloom of night. He said, "You make yourself sound like an Indian medicine man, Kell. You ride into a border gang's camp, talk a heathen killer out of a fortune in cattle, and ride out without getting any holes shot in your back. Anybody would be hard put to believe it."

"You calling me a liar now, Ira?"

"No. I'm turning it over in my mind."

Bennett ran a hand through his shaggy hair, trying to wipe away the anger that set his head throbbing. "You keep doing that, Ira. You can also keep remembering that I told you I know my way around up here. Garwood had heard of me, knew my reputation. He got the notion I aim to turn these cows over to my own boys, and that backed him off. I don't care how I get the best of these gangs, Ira. Whether you outsmart them or beat them off with a gun, you can whip them by pushing cattle past them."

He waited for Borden to nod, to show some sign of relief. When none came, the anger he had held in check exploded in his voice. Through gritted teeth, he said, "Don't hound me, Ira. What I've told you is on the level. You can stand there and fret all night if you want to but I'm going to sleep. We got by this time but somewhere up ahead the fight will come. You don't have to

149

keep looking for trouble. You're going to get your craw full of it."

Turning his back on Ira Borden, Bennett yanked at his blankets, rolled on his side, and left the gray old man standing with fury drawing his lips tight. But he did not relax until he heard the scuff of Borden's boots going away, then almost immediately he was asleep.

A rested body, a clear mind, and a man's thoughts become darting arrows, tracking back over a day and a night and picking up threads of reality which might have been dropped too hastily. In the misty light of dawn, Bennett reviewed his appraisal of Nelse Garwood and he was less content than he had been the night before.

It was possible that he had relied too strongly on instinct in judging the man. Garwood was a study of contrasts and contradictions. He was obviously a product of culture and education; still he had cast his lot with the ignorant and prejudiced, the killers and thieves. Few people had ever seen Nelse Garwood, but they knew his reputation around the saloons and dead-falls. He was known as the man who had slaughtered and stolen more Texas herds than any other.

Bennett clung to his faith in Garwood's word for one reason. Although the man's past was marked by ruth-lessness, he had shown many of the same symptoms Bennett himself had experienced. Garwood seemed bitter and disillusioned, a man nagged by remorse and regrets.

If the Horseshoe herd moved on unchallenged, Nelse Garwood had changed considerably. And Bennett had no choice but to put the man to this test.

He rushed the men through breakfast, keeping a

steady watch on the hills. He was the first man to rope a horse, the first to swing a lass rope and send the rousing cattle call over the herd.

Close behind him was Ira Borden. Silent and thoughtful, his leathery face as unrelenting as stone. Borden moved when Bennett Kell moved. Suspicion still pressed at Borden's mind, and he was keeping an eye on Bennett.

Out of the valley, the Horseshoe herd moved through a break in the knolls and pushed on to the north. Bennett breathed easier as the hours passed, and by noon he had almost forgotten Nelse Garwood. Again he settled down to the monotony of the drive, but his plainsman's gaze was forever sweeping ahead of the cattle. Each passing mile brought him closer to Kansas City and Ada McKittridge. And the same steps took him closer to Toby Rusk and a grudge which had to be settled. . . .

Three days took them out of the rolling hills and they drove across a sloping plain. Sight of the open country drew an exuberant yell from one of the Texans, and Bennett twisted in the saddle to look back at the men of the drive.

Behind them lay a month of trailing, a dozen river crossings and as many threats of stampede. Twice they had sighted far-off Indian parties, and a few days past the Red River they had made a gift of a crippled steer to a cadaverous Osage and his bedraggled squaw. There had been fights and arguments and constant tensions, but every man was still alive and the herd was safe. A dozen men and a lone woman had met the challenge of a raw land, and so far they held the upper hand.

In another three days they would be in Kansas City.

Ira Borden would open his gold cache and their wages would be paid. There would be money to spend, whisky to drink, women to kiss, and a time for a man to hold his head up high. And Shad Miller, the cotton-topped kid from the Big Bend, would be able to celebrate his birthday with a soft pillow beneath him and a roof over his head.

So a man had a right to shout if he felt like it. Only Bennett Kell and Ira Borden knew how close they had come to disaster at the hands of Nelse Garwood. The rest of the Horseshoe was beginning to believe they were living a miracle, and they wanted to shout their triumph.

There was laughter and talk and good-natured joshing around the fire that night. After Bonnie Gray had helped Cass clean up, she sat by the fire and sang a song for the crew. And as her throaty voice rose in a sentimental ballad, her hand clung to Wade Zumbro's.

Beside Bennett, Clay Macklin squatted on his heels and drew meaningless lines in the dirt with a twig. He pushed his hat back and his doleful, hound-dog face softened under a lopsided grin.

"I been thinking," he drawled, "about the first thing I'd buy when I hit town. I figure I'll buy me about four white shirts. That's one thing I ain't ever owned, is a white shirt. That's the first thing I aim to buy me."

"Not me," Bert Roscoe grinned. "The first thing I aim to buy is a wedding present for Bennett. He ain't told me yet, but I know there's a gal up here."

Bennett forced a smile. "I hope she's still around, Bert. And I hope the wedding present will be in order."

The talk went on, some of the men dreaming a little of the things they would do with money, others just

152

talking to use up time. They were confident, relaxed, and Bennett guessed they were counting on their luck again.

Day after day he had ridden among them with a grim face, warning them of the constant threat which weighed upon him like a curse. Until now nothing had happened, and he feared they were beginning to regard him as a false prophet of doom.

Tonight he made no attempt to rob them of this carefree hour, but he was moody and tense himself. He walked away from the fire, too restless to sit idle, and it was then that he saw a light flicker briefly out on the plain.

His first impulse was to call out an alarm so the others could verify his eyesight. But it was a bad time to create panic and confusion unless he was more certain help was needed. He wanted the crew to be ready at the right time, and false alarms dulled the edge of a man's vigilance.

Bennett checked the lay of the land with his eyes. To his right was the dark bulk of the bunched herd. But the flare of light had come from his left, farther north. It was only a speck in the night, and it could have been a firefly. But it looked more like the glow of a match being set hastily to a cigarette, and it was in the wrong direction to have been made by one of the nighthawks.

Bennett got his horse and rode casually away from the camp. A hundred yards toward the herd to satisfy the curiosity of anyone who might be watching, and then a quick swing northward. It was a slow, furtive ride. A hundred feet and a halt while Bennett dismounted and tramped through the knee-high grass, his eyes searching the ground. The moon was not yet up, but the sky was filled with glittering stars and a moving shadow would be spotted by probing eyes. It was a ride which could end with a shot in the dark and a bullet in the back, and Bennett could feel the skin tighten expectantly between his shoulder blades.

But he went steadily on, beginning a series of circles which drew narrowing rings about the general area in which he had seen the light. Leaning low beside his horse's neck, he stared at the ground until his eyes ached with strain. But at last he had his reward. He jerked suddenly at the reins, stepped to the ground and sank quickly to his knees. Here the grass was bent and matted. The shape of the depression showed where a man had lain and peered south toward the Horseshoe camp. Closer inspection revealed the spot where a horse had been picketed, and the tracks indicated a hasty retreat. Apparently the man had fled as soon as he saw Bennett ride into the open.

Scowling, he plucked a cigarette stub from the trampled sage and straightened. His hand plunged immediately toward his holstered gun, snapping it up to fire at the shadowy horseman moving in on him.

Almost too late he noticed the absence of a hat on the rider's head. He let his breath out in a nervous sigh, kept his eyes on the grizzled gray of the head.

"You do a lot of night riding," Ira Borden said, bringing his horse in close. "Can't you sleep?"

"Not when I figure I got a rifle aimed at my blankets. I thought I saw somebody out here a while ago. Looks like I was right."

A frown dug deep into Borden's craggy face. "When you smell trouble, Kell, you ought to holler at me. I could be some help, maybe."

154

The frosty glint was in Borden's eyes again. Since Bennett's lone ride to confer with Nelse Garwood, the rancher had been unable to trust him. He was no longer sure a man could slip into the mire and climb back to decency, and he was afraid Bennett was going to sell him out.

It showed in the cold tone of his voice and in his wary glance. Borden's manner sent anger tearing through Bennett. But it was part of the price he had to pay for his past, he decided, and fought his temper under control.

"This is no one-man drive," Borden said gruffly.

"When the right time comes I'll holler good and loud, Ira. Right now I don't want to upset the men. I figured it was a single scout and that's what it was."

Borden grunted. He inspected the broken grass, ran his gaze all around him, and shifted in the saddle. "It could have been an Indian waiting to steal a steer."

Bennett held out the cigarette stub for the rancher to see. "Indians don't roll much Bull Durham. This was white man's smoke, Ira."

"Who then?"

"Some of my old outfit, more than likely. It's my guess they've been watching us for days. If they know I'm with this herd they'll blow the lid off."

There was no change in the hard face. A vein throbbed in Borden's temple, and his heavy knuckles turned white under his fierce grip on the reins.

"We're getting close to the railhead," Borden said, turning his horse. "I'll drive day and night before I'll lose this herd. Anyway, they don't have much time to start anything."

"That's right," Bennett agreed. He mounted and

rode alongside the rancher. "But they'll start it just the same. You can bet all the gold you've got nailed to the floor of that buckboard they'll start it."

Borden made no reply and they rode on in silence. Bennett let his gaze run northward, thinking of the nearness of Kansas City. At the plodding pace of cattle, it was two days or more away. But a man on a fast horse could reach the town by daylight. The right man could hold lovely Ada McKittridge in his arms, kiss the warm lips and run his fingers through the soft gold of her hair. But was he the right man?

Not Bennett Kell. Not yet. He'd be no better than when he left her unless he rode in with a Texas herd.

His thoughts turned back to the broken grass and the man who had spied on the Horseshoe herd. A moment ago, with visions of Ada McKittridge's loveliness in his mind, Kansas City had seemed only a step away; but now the railhead was like a taunting mirage, as distant as the other side of the world.

Toby Rusk was on the move. He had his scouts out to check the herd Bennett had promised to drive to Missouri, and somewhere in the darkness the burly raider would be drawing plans for an attack.

Ada McKittridge looked at the arching sky and played a guessing game with the stars which glittered brightly over Kansas City. She played the game often when she was thinking of Bennett Kell.

Somewhere to the south, over a land as big and trackless as the sky above it, she knew the sun-browned Texan was riding this way. Perhaps his eyes and hers would touch the same star. It was her way of trying to draw him close, to wipe out the distance between them so she could imagine that she might see his face or hear his voice at any minute.

Her heel struck a crack in the crude sidewalk, and her uncle's strong arm clutched at her as she stumbled. "You certainly seem preoccupied this evening, my dear," Big Jim McKittridge said. "You've scarcely spoken to poor Dillman since we left the hotel."

Ada smiled apologetically at the slender, blond young man on her left. "Please forgive me, Ed. I suppose I am terribly dull when I'm in one of my melancholy moods."

"What she means, Ed," McKittridge said with a wink at the man, "is that she's still mooning over that handsome Texan she met a month or so ago. I'm counting on you to improve her disposition some while I'm away."

A chiding chuckle hummed through McKittridge's words, but it broke off under a disapproving glance from his niece. McKittridge jammed his cigar into his mouth and strode on in silence.

Ada felt Ed Dillman's eyes studying her covertly, and she slipped her arm impulsively through his. It was more of a delaying tactic than a show of affection and it allowed her to concentrate on her own thoughts without interruption.

Ed Dillman had been in Kansas City for two weeks and it seemed that McKittridge had made every excuse to throw him and Ada together as much as possible. And now McKittridge was leaving town for two days, riding over to Kansas to check the progress of the railroad. He had made a show of asking Dillman to see that Ada was adequately protected while he was away.

Until now Ada had refused to face the suspicion which had been growing in her mind. Big Jim McKittridge liked young men with ambition and promise, men with a taste for fine clothes and a well-turned phrase. Ed Dillman, two years out of law school and already on the railroad's legal staff, qualified for McKittridge's approval. At first Ada had thought her uncle's interest went no deeper than one man's admiration for another, but now she was not certain. Big Jim McKittridge, she suspected, was trying to crowd the memory of Bennett Kell from her mind, hoping to find her a husband before Bennett could meet the standards McKittridge had set for him.

Moved by impulse, Ada stopped abruptly and tugged at her uncle's arm. "I'm not going to let you leave me, Uncle Jim. I'm sure there's nothing so pressing that you must ride out at night. You can wait until morning and I'll ride with you."

McKittridge's ruddy face registered a brief surprise, and he was able to read more in the girl's accusing tone than he was from her words. Ada looked extremely feminine and helpless in a blue-checked gingham dress, and McKittridge frowned in irritation as two overalled men passed them and turned to stare at her.

"I'll never try to lie to you or deceive you, my dear," McKittridge said humbly. "We're having some trouble getting out timber at our first way station, and I'll be able to get to the root of that problem before the night is over. It's only a few miles. Farther on there's some confusion over rights-of-way, and I can investigate that tomorrow if I'm prepared to leave the way station at daybreak. I'm rushing myself, Ada, so I won't have to leave you alone in this town too long."

Ada was touched by the sincerity in the big man's eyes, and she was suddenly ashamed. She smiled and touched McKittridge's thick arm. "I'm sorry, Uncle Jim. Your work must be done, and I suppose I shouldn't be so selfish. You go right ahead, and I won't worry any more. I promise."

Ed Dillman touched her arm reassuringly. "There'll be no cause for you to worry, Ada. My room is next to your suite, and I promise to sleep with one eye open until Mr. McKittridge returns."

"Good boy, Ed!" McKittridge said heartily. "I'm counting on that."

They walked on to the livery stable, threading through the constant rush of traffic that milled between the railroad yard and the higher levels of the city. Farther on, the music and boisterous laughter of the saloon district gave the city a rowdy, bawdy atmosphere that always made Ada conscious of the difference in this land and the home she had known in Philadelphia.

While McKittridge made arrangements to rent a horse she waited at the edge of the corrals with Ed Dillman. After a few attempts at conversation Dillman fell silent and Ada found herself studying the stars again.

She became conscious of eyes upon her and reached automatically for the protection of Dillman's arm. Two men had followed them up the slope. They stood on the other side of the corral now, boldly appraising the compact curves of Ada's slender form. Light from the lantern swinging over the livery's double doors splashed across the intent faces and an involuntary shudder skipped along Ada's spine.

"Do you know them?" Ed Dillman asked indignantly,

following the girl's gaze.

"No—no, I was just startled to see them there."

Dillman tugged thoughtfully at the lapels of his salt-and-pepper coat. "Then I'll ask them to move along. It isn't very polite of them to stand and leer at you this way."

"No!" Ada's voice was a taut whisper. She grabbed at Dillman's hand as he started away, pulling him back. She forced a laugh. "You must get accustomed to Kansas City, Ed. If it weren't for things like this I might forget I am a woman."

Ada was grateful for McKittridge's return. The railroader got out of the saddle to kiss her cheek and pat Ed Dillman's shoulder. Then he was gone in a flurry of hoofbeats.

"See you in two days for sure," McKittridge called over his shoulder.

Pretending another interest in the sky, Ada stole a glance at the two loungers nearby. She felt relieved when they moved away, walking hurriedly toward the yawning doors of the livery stable.

Going back to the hotel, Ada kept up a constant chatter all the way. She was trying to shut out the memory of the men at the livery but idle talk would jot push away the apprehension built in her by the sight of them. She kept seeing their faces in her mind. One of the men was thick-bodied, with a short neck that made his head appear to set directly against his shoulders. In the lantern light, she had seen the two deep shadows which marked the dimples in his broad face. The other man was thin and quick-moving, as dark and graceful as a panther.

Although she had been truthful when she told Ed

Dillman she did not know the men, Ada had withheld the fact that she had seen them before. Once she had spotted them sulking in the shadows behind the hotel after one of her secret meetings with Bennett. When she mentioned their suspicious behavior to Bennett he had guessed their identity by the descriptions she gave and his face had turned gray with anger. In answer to her questions Bennett had told her they were a couple of ruffians named Toby Rusk and Wally Bryan.

Feeling a dread at being alone, Ada made the evening last as long as possible. She accepted Dillman's invitation for a late snack in the hotel dining room, lingering over her coffee and turning an attentive face to the young lawyer's quiet conversation.

"It's wonderful to sit and talk with you like this, Ada," Dillman said earnestly. "I hope we may spend night after night like this, and one day perhaps . . ."

Ada smiled appreciatively, understanding the implication of the unfinished sentence. Mentally she compared the handsome, dapper young man with the dark, rough-spoken Texan who had ridden in from nowhere to claim a place in her life.

Perhaps it was this sharp contrast which had aroused Ada's interest at their first meeting. Most of her adult life had been spent across tables from suave, polished men like Ed Dillman. She had observed the wives of such men, pondering their very proper and very useless lives, and her heart had cried out against the curse which had made her a woman. Then Ada had met Bennett Kell, and she had sensed no such rebellion within herself since that meeting.

Her heart had raced with excitement when she met him, and she knew the thrill of his presence would not subside during a lifetime at his side. A woman could see in Bennett Kell more than the rugged handsomeness of his face, more than the breath-taking sweep of his shoulders. She saw a man as big and bold as the land which had bred him, a man who would conquer this land and make it grow. And the woman who shared his life would have a part in all this, a usefulness which Ada McKittridge had always known must be hers.

A teasing voice interrupted her thoughts. "You've got that look in your eyes again," Ed Dillman said. "The one you have when you study the stars."

Ada smiled. "I must be tired, Ed. It's past my bedtime, you know."

Ed Dillman hurried to her chair, as attentive as a mother hen. He helped Ada to her feet, guided her elbow lightly as they climbed the stairs to the McKittridge suite. Ada bade him good night at her door, but Dillman insisted on coming inside to light a lamp and check the rooms for intruders.

In the first fluttering flare of the match Ada saw the man sitting on the edge of the leather-cushioned chair. A scream rose in her throat, but there was a quick move behind her and a thin hand clamped against her mouth, stifling the sound.

"Go ahead and light the lamp, buster," Toby Rusk growled at Ed Dillman. "When you do just keep your hands up there close to the roof."

Dillman's fingers trembled, but he finally managed to set the wick aflame. As light flooded the room Toby Rusk stepped out and swung his gun at the lawyer's head. Its barrel made a crunching sound. A spot of blood appeared at the edge of Dillman's straw-colored hair, and he wilted to the floor.

"Now turn the gal loose, Wally," Toby Rusk said. "She'll listen to reason unless she wants some of the same."

Wally Bryan's arms dropped away, but Toby Rusk had misjudged Ada McKittridge. Her gray eyes flashed desperately around the room, and then she charged furiously at Toby Rusk. Sharp-toed shoes kicked at his shins and long-fingered nails clawed at his bearded face.

Wally Bryan was only a step away. He grabbed at the collar of her dress. Ada wrenched aside, ignoring the ripping sound as the cloth tore away. Then Wally Bryan's vise-like fingers found her hands, drawing both of them behind her and high-between her shoulders.

"You dirty brutes," Ada breathed scornfully. "You'll have Big Jim McKittridge after you if you touch me, and the world won't be big enough for you to hide in."

"You're scaring me to death," Toby Rusk growled. He took a folded neck scarf from his hip pocket, slapped it across Ada's mouth and tied the ends at the back of her neck.

Rusk's eyes clung to the creamy white of Ada's bare shoulder and he let his hand slide lightly across the tear in her dress. He stepped back, his lips parted in a damp grin.

"Get something around her hands, Wally," he said, "and let's get her down the back steps before somebody hears all the ruckus up here. Here's where Bennett Kell learns it don't pay to try to be a big shot."

Fifteen

It was a bad day from the start. Shad Miller almost broke his neck and the drive was delayed for nearly an hour.

Shad's trouble could be charged to the impulses of youth. He was drawing his horse from the remuda, but he couldn't keep his eyes off Bonnie Gray. The girl had already taken her place on the seat of the supply wagon which she had occupied alone since the night she had fought with Ira Borden. Her fresh, clear beauty glowed in the soft light of pre-dawn, and the provocative curves of her body were clearly outlined in the tight levis and gaudy yellow blouse she had chosen to wear.

Saddle balanced on his shoulder, Shad led his horse near the wagon to work with the gear. Around him, the rest of the crew was doing the same and only Bennett Kell, already mounted and waiting, was aware that Shad was showing off.

At first it did not disturb him. Bonnie's saloon life was behind her and she had learned that the flirtatious tricks which made a dry cattleman buy more drinks had a different effect on men grown tired of their own company. She gave Shad only casual attention, and perhaps it was her unconcern which spurred him to recklessness.

He tightened the cinch and stepped back a few paces from the prancing bronc. Then he broke into a short, choppy run. A springy leap, two hands shoved against the horse's rump, and Shad vaulted into the saddle.

A man more experienced with a range horse's nature would not have tried such a trick. Shad stayed in the saddle long enough to flash a quick smile at Bonnie. Then the horse whirled in a half-spin, threw Shad off balance, and shot its heels toward the heavens. Shad was flipped from the saddle like a weight from a catapult. He sailed past Bonnie and landed against Cass Bailey's chuck wagon a dozen feet away. His head made a cracking noise as it struck the rear wheel.

He lay still, one arm twitching feebly. Bennett swore and jumped to the ground. He looked at the youngster's quiet face, felt the egg-sized bump on Shad's head, and put an ear to the bony chest to listen for life.

Bonnie touched his arm. "Is—is he dead, Bennett?"

"No. But he may be bad hurt. We'll see."

"Maybe we ought to put him in the supply wagon." Wade Zumbro knelt at Bennett's side. He had his hat in his hand, twisting nervously at the brim, and Bennett was surprised to see the earnest concern in his face.

A shadow fell across them. Ira Borden shouldered his way through the huddled crew. He said, "Leave his horse standing with him and mount up. When he comes to he can catch up."

"We'll wait and see if he's going to live, Borden. If he

dies out here they'll be nobody to dig a grave. We'll wait."

There was a finality in Bennett's words. He raised his eyes to meet Borden's frosty glance, held them there until the rancher's rigid shoulders relaxed. Borden folded his arms, set his back against the rim of the far wheel and looked away.

Bonnie pushed her way forward with a pan of water she had drawn from the drinking barrel on the side of the wagon. Her slender hands dipped into the water, and she rubbed Shad's forehead gently. She loosened the youngster's shirt and bathed his chest, and presently Shad's eyes fluttered open.

For a moment he lay that way, remembering, and then he grinned boyishly. Pushing Bonnie aside, he started to sit up. But his glance shifted abruptly and his narrow eyes grew large. His lips moved silently and the finger he pointed beneath the wagon shook with excitement.

"Look—look at that!" Shad stammered. "It's a gold piece!"

The others looked and a startled silence fell over them. There in the grass, just beyond the rim of the wagon wheel, lay a glittering double eagle.

A choked sound came from Ira Borden's throat. He fell to his knees, shoving the men aside, and a strange look passed over his rawboned face. Clutching fingers stabbed at the grass and Ira Borden grabbed the coin. Beneath the wagon he went, cuffing his flopping black hat away from his face. He twisted to inspect the wagon bed. Near the far edge, a seam had widened enough to allow a single coin to slip through.

Borden stayed on the ground, bawling orders. Cass

166

Bailey tore a strip from a cartridge case and brought it to him, holding the nails between his teeth. With the end of a running iron, Borden nailed the strip fast, tested it with his powerful hands, and backed into the open.

He rose slowly. Sweat beaded his seamed face. He set his hands on his hips and ran his cold eyes over the faces around him. "Now you know where it is. But that's where it stays until we load these cattle. Anybody think different?"

Not a sound from the crew. The rasping voice had jarred the surprise out of them and now the men were shuffling restlessly. Shad Miller was the first to move, saying meekly, "I reckon I've held things up long enough."

Only Bonnie still looked stunned, and Bennett could guess what she was thinking. She had come close to trading her respect for a look at the gold, and every night she had slept only a few feet away from it.

As he rode past her on his way to take his place at point the girl said, "Shad was lucky, wasn't he?"

"Maybe," Bennett said, wondering how she meant the remark. Maybe she meant Shad's narrow escape—and maybe she meant his discovery of the gold.

The Horseshoe's luck ran out that day at sunset. Their progress had been slow and fretful and Borden had given up in exasperation. He called for an early camp after the cattle had balked, for no apparent reason, at crossing a narrow river. Most of the afternoon had been spent in forcing them across. They came out on a level strip of land at the foot of a row of low hills, and Borden did not want to risk passing the suitable bed ground.

He said, "We can mark off another lost day. We're

still two days from the railroad."

Borden stamped away, leaving his horse standing where Ben Lufton was bunching the remuda. The wrangler looked at Bennett and shook his head.

"He's always talking two ways at once, that man," Lufton said. "These cows won't be moved in the dark no more. Borden can't keep his eye on that chuck wagon good enough if it's moving. Now that we know where he hid his gold he—"

Lufton left the remark dangling as the rest of the crew rode in to leave their horses. Bennett took time to search for his own dun in the riding string, found it looking fit after a rest. Satisfied, he started toward the chuck wagon, sniffing the odors that were already coming from Cass Bailey's fire.

A few paces behind him were the other riders, grunting with weariness and cursing the troubles of the day. It was their sudden silence which first alerted Bennett, and he lifted his gaze abruptly.

His heart thumped hollowly against his ribs. Directly ahead of him, silhouetted against the crest of a bare hill, was a long line of horsemen. They had drawn rein there, sitting like statues carved against the sky, and Bennett had time to count them.

Twenty men! Twenty men strung out as though ready for a charge, and Bennett could see a rifle braced casually across the pommel of each saddle.

Ira Borden saw them too. His booming voice speared across the land, ordering the Horseshoe to load their guns and stand ready to fire. Borden was coming toward them in a stiff-gaited run, his arms waving with each command.

"Keep your shirt on, Ira," Bennett yelled sharply.

And to the men behind him: "Just sit tight until we see what's going on. We don't want to start a fight we can't finish. They outnumber us nearly two to one."

"Looks like they're sending somebody out to palaver," Scrap Dooley said quietly.

A single rider detached himself from the others and sent his horse jogging down the slope. The last yellow rays of the sun glistened brightly against a patch of metal on the wiry rider's leg, and Bennett's mouth felt dry. That bright spot would be the nickel-plated gun Wally Bryan always wore.

"What do you make of it, Kell?" Borden stopped beside him, his breath wheezing. "Is this the showdown you've been talking about?"

Bennett kept his eyes on the approaching rider. "I don't know what they're up to, Ira. But I know this. The man coming in is Wally Bryan. He used to work for me." He paused, gestured at the Colt in Borden's fist. "I'd put that away, Ira. Wally's the fastest thing I've ever seen with a gun, and I wouldn't want to push him."

Borden took a quick look around him, checking the number of men behind him. He holstered the gun, spread his feet wide and turned defiantly to face the rider.

A dozen feet in front of the bunched cowboys Wally Bryan brought his prancing black to a standstill. He folded his long-fingered hands on the saddlehorn, leaned forward to peer at the standing men.

"Hello, Bennett," he said in his purring voice. His sharp chin moved with the words, but his thin lips stayed close together, hiding the emptiness of his tooth-less mouth. "I see you came back."

169

Bennett nodded. "You knew I'd be back, Wally."

"That was a mistake. Rusk sent me down to tell you this is far as you go. We mean to take these cattle."

From the corner of his eye, Bennett saw Ira Borden's feet move. He flung a restraining arm across the rancher's waist, took a step forward.

"That's a point we'll argue, Wally."

Wally Bryan glanced over his shoulder toward the line of silent horsemen. "We've picked up some help since you left us," he murmured.

"I expected that of Rusk. He wants to be a big man. But you won't find it as easy as it was in the old days, Wally. We won't run when you start the stampede. I'm here with this crew, and I know the tricks you'll try. We'll be throwing lead, Wally. Go tell Rusk he's got a fight on his hands."

The hint of a smile stretched across Wally Bryan's tight mouth. He shook his head from side to side, his china-blue eyes alive with a secret fire. "You ain't going to fight, Bennett. We're playing a hole card you can't beat."

Wally Bryan twisted in the saddle, shoved a hand into the pocket of his patched moleskin. He kept his palm closed, and when he looked back at Bennett the pale eyes were as hard as polished stone.

"Remember that woman you was so wild about in Kansas City, Bennett? Rusk and I been keeping an eye on her. Yesterday that big shot McKittridge had to ride over into Kansas to see how the railroad's coming along. He told the liveryman he wouldn't be back till tomorrow." Rusk waved a white hand, impatient with the details. "We've got the girl, Bennett. If you want her back, call off these Texas guns. Pull this crew back out

170

of shooting range, and we'll come down after the cattle."

Bennett stared incredulously at the sallow-faced ex-gambler. His stomach turned sick, and his chest swelled with hopeless fury.

"You're lying, Wally. Rusk knows you can end up on a hangrope when you start stealing women."

Wally Bryan did not argue. He held out his clenched fist, palm upward, and slowly unfolded his fingers. A wisp of golden color, held together with a short raw-hide string, showed in his hand. A wave of Wally's arm sent the object into the air, and Bennett reached out to catch it. He held the rawhide string and stared at the small lock of hair, watching the color of it come alive in the sunset. Wally Bryan needed to say nothing more.

Panic and fury filled Bennett Kell's mind. He wanted to drive a hand at his gun, to blast the life from the smug, ruthless man who had brought him this message. But Wally Bryan's death would not free Ada. It would not foil Toby Rusk's pledge to keep Bennett out of Missouri. It would not save the Horseshoe herd.

A snort of rage burst from Ira Borden. He strode toward Wally Bryan, a hand on his gun, and for the first time Bennett realized the decision was not his to make. To save Ada McKittridge he would surrender his life, the ranch on the Brazos and all other things he owned. But the Horseshoe herd belonged to Ira Borden, and Borden was not a man to surrender anything.

Desperately, Bennett stepped across to block Borden's path. He showed Wally Bryan a calm face, a strained smile. "There's not much your kind of scum won't do, Wally, but I don't figure you'd kill a woman

171

just because we won't hand over this herd."

Wally Bryan shrugged. He lifted the horse's reins as if to go. "Who said anything about killing a gal like Ada McKittridge? If you make us fight, Rusk figures to keep her around for a few days and have a little fun. By the time McKittridge gets hot on our trail we'll be through with her."

Sixteen

The strained smile dwindled from Bennett's face. The blood drained from his lips, and his dark eyes were dull with defeat. He thought of Toby Rusk's dirty, sweating body crushing the resistance from a helpless woman.

He turned a desperate look at the crew, but he could find no answer to his dilemma in their bewildered faces. Only Bonnie Gray seemed to comprehend the panic that had swept abruptly through Bennett Kell. He had not heard her arrive, but curiosity apparently had drawn her here from the wagons. She stood only a few feet away, a compassionate expression in her eyes.

Suddenly she stepped around Ira Borden's broad back and clutched at Bennett's arm. She leaned her head against his shoulder and a soft hand touched his cheek.

"Don't listen to him, darling!" Bonnie Gray said tearfully. "I know you still feel you owe something to that girl you met up there, but you can't let it ruin our lives. Please, Bennett, don't do anything to take us apart. Let him keep the girl. She means nothing to you now."

Puzzled at first by the girl's outburst, understanding came to Bennett, and he slipped his arm around her slender waist. He held to the girl and watched Wally's face for signs of doubt, grateful at last for Bonnie's presence.

The mounted man's eyes studied the girl's face briefly, running over her swelling breasts and flaring hips. Wally Bryan shook his head slowly. "You're putting on a show, girlie. Kell wouldn't throw over the McKittridge girl for you. You ain't got enough class."

She stamped her foot indignantly, stepped close to the raider's horse. "If I could reach you, I'd slap your face, mister! Bennett and I are going to be married in Kansas City, and you can throw that Ada girl to the wolves for all he cares!"

A chuckle sounded deep in Wally Bryan's chest. He slid from the saddle and faced Bonnie Gray. Without warning, he grabbed her around the waist, his wide mouth searching for her lips while his free hand pawed over the curves of her body.

There was a movement behind Bennett Kell. Wade Zumbro pushed forward, uttering a low curse. "Turn her loose, damn you," Zumbro yelled, "or I'll kill you where you stand!"

In a single graceful move, Wally Bryan flung the girl away from him and drew his gun. He waved Zumbro back and shoved the girl along with him. The lightning speed of the man quieted the crew, and Bennett was left facing him alone again.

Holstering the shiny Colt, Wally climbed calmly back into the saddle. "It didn't work, Bennett. There's

174

always a way to find out who a woman belongs to. Let's get back to business."

"I'm obliged to you, Bonnie," Bennett said quietly. Then to Wally Bryan: "I've heard half of the bargain. What's the rest of it?"

"We'll turn the girl loose in Kansas City. She won't be harmed." Wally Bryan paused. "If it'll make you feel better, I don't like any part of it. If you'll pull your men away from the herd, I'll see that the girl stays safe. Otherwise, I'll stand by Toby Rusk."

A heavy hand shoved Bennett aside before he could reply to the terms. Ira Borden glared at Wally Bryan, his neck muscles knotted with fury. "I've listened long enough. Get out, rustler. Get out before I lay my hands on you. Nobody gives these cows away to buy a woman we never saw in our lives."

"You're wrong, Ira." Bennett Kell's hand flicked down and up, and the muzzle of his gun pressed against the rancher's broad back. "That woman stays alive. She's going to stay safe if it takes every cow in Texas."

Before Borden could recover from his surprise, Bennett's hand darted to the man's holster. He lifted the big .44, flung it away into the grass. Then he stepped back so he could see the others.

"That's the way it is, men," he said. "If you don't want to take my orders, make your fight now."

Ira Borden barked orders at the crew, the bellowing voice echoing across the land in a mixture of pleas and curses. But not a man moved. They ignored Ira Borden. One at a time they met Bennett's gaze, nodded their heads in assent.

"All right, Wally," he said. "You can take Rusk the

word. But if you plan to harm her, you better kill me now. I'll hunt you down, Wally."

No answer came from Wally Bryan. His lips twitched in that hint of a smile and he rode toward the hills much faster than he had come.

"You mean to keep that bargain, Kell?" Ira Borden faced Bennett, his fists clenched at his sides.

"I do. Don't pick up that gun, Ira, and don't try to interfere when they come for the cattle. Later I'll—"

Bennett left the sentence unfinished. Ira Borden's clubby right hand snatched at his flopping hat. He tossed it on the ground, and the sound of its falling could be heard in the sudden stillness.

Borden eyed Bennett Kell from beneath tufted brows. A bright, irrational gleam flickered in his pale eyes. He made a spitting motion at each of his palms, rubbed them together and strode toward Bennett.

"You've gone too far, Kell." Borden's guttural voice held the tone of an executioner. "You may look big as a barn and wild as a bear to those men, but not to me. I'm going to beat you until you can't stand, by God, and then I'm going to stomp you into the dirt!"

Bennett, who had holstered his own gun, scowled incredulously as Borden crouched and raised his fists. It was not Ira Borden's way to prove his strength in a common brawl. His was an inner steel, a force to be read from the fiber of his voice, the flint of his eyes and the fearless defiance of all threats to his hard will. A loss of face, a jolt to the fierce dignity, and Ira Borden's power would be lost.

Borden's rage had made him blind to these things. He planted his feet and swung a terrific blow at Bennett. A lifted arm blocked the fist, but Bennett felt

176

the shock of it run through his arms and shoulders. He danced away from Borden, his face still clouded with concern.

Twice he had fought against his will on this drive, and now a greater principle was involved. Only as a last resort could he strike the man he'd sworn to protect. Especially when that man was twice his age.

Ira Borden goaded Bennett with taunts and threats. "With gray in my hair and frost in my bones I'll be a better man than you, Kell! You may turn your tail and run, but you won't get away."

Borden came at him again. Bennett braced momentarily, anger welling within him. The rancher towered above him, a giant of a man with muscles bulging every seam of his clothing. The difference in weight would balance the difference in age, Bennett thought angrily, and cocked his fist. But as Borden came within striking range, he let his arm relax.

He said hurriedly, "I don't want to fight you, Ira. It's a waste for both of us. Let's talk—"

He held his ground too long, and Borden's great arms enveloped him. He was crushed against Borden's chest, and a savage pressure grew against his back. The rancher's arms tightened. A blunt chin dug into Bennett's chest, bending him backward like a sapling. He gasped for air, and suddenly his lungs were too tortured to accept it. His breath stopped and bright specks danced across his vision.

He shoved desperately against Borden's shoulders, but it was like pushing at a mountain. At last he let his legs grow limp, lifting his toes to put all his weight in the man's arms. Borden's iron grip slipped, and Bennett wrenched himself free.

His own momentum threw him to the ground. He fell on his side, his mouth agape as he drank in refreshing air. Dimly, he heard a warning yell from the crew. He raised his head, blinking to clear his vision. Borden's scuffed boot was raised high for a kick. Bennett rolled aside, and the man's boot heel scraped skin from his ribs.

Borden's age did not show in his quick steps. He strode to Bennett's side, bending at the waist to swing his fist. The blow smashed against Bennett's nose, sent blood spurting across his face. Borden braced for another, but Bennett ducked and bounded to his feet.

Again he backed away. "I'm not going to fight you, Ira! Don't make me pull out and leave you in a spot like this."

Borden answered with a rush. In his haste to retreat, Bennett tripped over his own spur. He fell clumsily and Borden's boot lifted for another kick.

It was then that one of the Horseshoe riders grabbed Borden's shirt collar, pulling him back. Ben Lufton snatched at an arm, and in a moment the rancher was held helplessly at bay.

"Lay off, Ira," Ben Lufton said, and the wrangler's drawl was a husky threat. "What's done is done, and killing each other ain't likely to change it. Bennett could likely salivate you with his fists, but he said he didn't want to fight you. Now, lay off or fight us all."

Gradually Borden's struggles subsided. The restraining hands dropped away and he turned his back on the crowd. He bent and retrieved his hat, set it squarely on his grizzled head. His eyes dwelled for a while on the gun which Bennett had taken from him and thrown into the grass. Then Borden straightened and stalked off toward the cook fire.

Afterward Bennett sat in the grass for a long time, filling his burning lungs with air and relaxing. He sleeved the blood from his nose and shook his head worriedly at Borden's broad back.

He had not expected help from the crew but he was grateful for their interference. He pushed to his feet, nodding his thanks to the quiet group near by. They had given him more comfort than they could guess. He had been afraid they might try to stop Toby Rusk's men from taking the cattle, although such a move would jeopardize Ada McKittridge's life. But now he knew where their loyalties lay.

Bennett picked up Ira Borden's cedar-handled .44 and stuffed it into his waistband. Still silent and thoughtful, he led off toward the wagons. The next two hours would be the worst of his life. Until darkness fell he would have to sit idly and pretend that Toby Rusk had completely thwarted him. But he had no intention of giving up so easily. Bonnie Gray had found a weakness which Bennett meant to pursue. Without a captive to barter with, Rusk's scheme was useless.

The murmur of voices behind him brought Bennett's thoughts back to the present. He stopped and looked around, disliking the tone of the talk.

"What's the complaint about?" he asked sharply.

Luke Ashley, the squat, dour night wrangler who seldom spoke, was doing most of the talking now. He shrugged his meaty shoulders. "I was just telling these fellers we might as well pull out for home tonight. It's a long way back, and I don't want to take as long going as I did coming. The moon will be up and we could ride a far piece tonight."

"Nobody rides anywhere tonight, Luke. That would fix everything fine. Right now I need you men worse than I've ever needed you. First, I aim to find my girl. When I know she's safe, we'll get that herd back."

"That's a big order," Wade Zumbro murmured. "Cattle are easier to give away than they are to take away from folks."

Color flooded Bennett Kell's face. The old belligerance was in Zumbro's tone and his mouth held a sullen droop. Bennett took a short step toward the rocky puncher.

"We've had enough fights," Bonnie Gray said sharply, and her eyes flashed equal scorn at Zumbro and Kell.

Bennett stifled his anger and walked on. He heard whispers at his back and the men split apart in small groups. It was a danger signal that put new uneasiness in his mind. The loyalties he had felt so strongly a few minutes ago were slipping away from him and he knew no way to retain them.

Seventeen

Twenty horsemen came down from the bare hills at dusk. They broke into small groups, circling the herd in different directions, scouting for a possible ambush.

Afterward they uncoiled ropes and flicked them at the cattle. The herd moved sluggishly, bawling its protest, and a dust cloud lifted up from the grass and floated across the hills.

As a single man, the Horseshoe crew stopped their eating and rose to their feet. Not a single word was spoken until the gray mass of the herd drifted across the flat and turned out of sight around the foothills.

Only Ira Borden had refused to move. He sat in his usual place, his back wedged against the wheel of the chuck wagon, and he ate with his usual vigor. Once his fork stopped midway between the plate and his mouth while his frosty eyes locked with Bennett's glance. Only that, and Borden said nothing as the border gang moved the herd off the bed ground and drove it north.

The men took their seats, but the unusual silence left in the herd's wake made them fidget and shift from

181

place to place. Somebody started toying with a six-gun, spinning the cylinder noisily, and Bennett knew what the men were thinking. It had been too easy, and it left shame in all who had witnessed the scene.

Rusk's orders had been followed in every detail. Borden had carried word of the terms to Cass Bailey at the wagons, and when Bennett arrived the cook had eyed him questioningly. Bennett had picked a new site, the wagons had been moved obediently, and every man had stayed in his place.

But they were restless now, drifting away from the fire by twos and threes to talk among themselves. Bennett sat at the edge of the ragged circle around the fire, giving his attention to his plate again. The food was tasteless, but he needed to keep busy at something. He did not want the others to see the nervous trembling of his hands or read the constant fear that might show in his face.

At last Bennett took his plate to the water barrel, rinsed it and set it on the tailgate. Cass Bailey put it in its place, saying, "You tried, Bennett. Nobody blames you for what you done."

"You know better than that, Cass," Bennett murmured and walked beyond the wagon. He reached for a cigar, his hand dropping away as he remembered he had smoked them all. There was a sack of stale tobacco in his saddlebags, but he did not consider going back for it.

He did not want to face the defeat-filled glances that would be turned his way. At his back the murmurings were still going on in subdued tones. They were talking about him, he thought ruefully, and they were entitled to do it out of earshot. Talk might do them good. There was a mood among them which Bennett could not quite identify, but he did not like it. A sense of foreboding nagged at him. Until the men had it talked out, whatever it was, it would be useless to talk to them or to ask for help. And he needed their help desperately.

A flurry of movement drew his attention back to the camp. Wade Zumbro had been huddled with a group of men some distance away from the fire. Now he came striding forward, his shoulders squared belligerently. He stopped in front of Ira Borden, and the others spread out around him. Monte Cole, Scrap Dooley, Luke Ashley. All had the same look as Zumbro, half-angry, half-afraid.

Bennett frowned, his eyes switching from Zumbro to Bert Roscoe. Roscoe had been with them in the huddle, but he had broken away as they approached Ira Borden. Now the red-haired puncher was circling among the men who were still seated around the fire. A hurried whisper beside each tilted hat, a furtive look, and Roscoe continued his rounds. Bennett hurried forward and Roscoe circled to avoid him.

Zumbro was speaking and his husky voice was loud enough for all to hear. "This is payday, Ira," Zumbro said flatly. "We stuck with you while you had a herd. That was our bargain. We rounded up them cattle on the Trinity and took your promise for back wages and trail drive money. Now pay us, Ira. Dig up that gold you've got hid and pay us off. There's no reason to wait longer."

"Hold it, Zumbro!" Bennett Kell stepped around to stand at Borden's side. "This drive isn't over. Borden's deal was to pay you off in Kansas City."

Zumbro shook his head impatiently. "Keep out of

this, Kell. We've got nothing to wait for. The herd is gone."

"We'll get it back. They won't drive it far by night. Give me a chance to find Ada, and I'll see that we get the herd back. I think I know where to find her. As soon as it's full dark, I figure I can get to her. That's what I've been waiting for." The words burst from Bennett in a single breath and there was a note of pleading in his voice.

Zumbro was unmoved. "All I've been waiting for is my money," he said stubbornly. "And now I aim to have it."

Ira Borden stood with his back against the chuck wagon. His hand touched his holster, found it empty, and his eyes went to Bennett Kell. The big gun was still stuffed in Bennett's waistband.

"You want to give me my gun now?" the rancher asked.

"No. I'll do as much as you, Ira. The gold stays where it is."

Bennett studied the faces ringed about him, and he could read nothing from them. He said, "The men won't stand with you, Zumbro. They'll do as I say, and then it'll be you and me."

"And me," Monte Cole said. Hand on his gun, the stringy old cowboy came forward to stand beside Zumbro.

Scrap Dooley, Bert Roscoe and Luke Ashley took a step closer to show their sentiments. Bennett held his breath and waited, sensing hesitation in the others. But only for a moment. Shad Miller moved in with the crew, and then Clay Macklin slipped in behind, his eyes downcast. At last only Cass Bailey and Ben Lufton

184

stood apart from the others. Bennett raised his eyes questioningly, and Ben Lufton looked at the ground.

"You too, Ben?" he asked softly.

"Me too," Lufton said, and took his stand with Zumbro. "The money's coming to me."

Cass Bailey's ferret eyes flicked across the hard-set faces beside him. He took a step toward the crew, paused, and kept coming until he stood beside Ira Borden.

"Twenty years is a long time to work for a man," he said. "I reckon it gets to be a habit, Ira."

Behind the crew, Bonnie Gray stood with hands clasped nervously, her face pale and strained while she waited to see the outcome. There was nervousness in the others, too. They had seen Bennett Kell at work with his fists and with his gun.

It was a time for breathing and nothing more. A single word, a quick move, and blood would be spilled. Bennett Kell could reach for his gun, and someone would die. Against such odds, he could not win; but he had the speed to demand a costly victory. Or he could shrug his shoulders and back away, and there would be no graves to dig.

And this was the choice he made. He let his shoulders go limp, cast a warning glance at Cass Bailey, and said, "There's an axe in the wood box. You know where the gold is."

Wood splintered, the axe clanged, and the false floor of the chuck wagon was chopped away. Ben Lufton did the counting, sorting the gold pieces and taking each man's word for his wages. Afterward there was the bustle of men assembling their gear, and Wade Zumbro called to Bonnie Gray.

The Horseshoe crew was going home, back to Texas. Zumbro and Bonnie rode with them. The trail drive had taught Zumbro patience, and he was no longer sure that Texas was doomed. He had not liked what he saw of Missouri, and the jingle of money in his pockets gave him confidence. There would be time for a wedding in Texas.

A flurry of hoofs, a blossom of dust, and eight men rode south. Bennett made no attempt to stop them. They knew he needed them, knew he would make an effort to regain the herd if they stayed. He had told them that the minute Wally Bryan had made his bargain and rode away. But still the men rode home, leaving him with a scrawny cook and a rancher who had been robbed of all he owned.

And Borden held Bennett responsible for his loss. Unarmed and helpless, the rancher had held his silence while the rebellion ran its course. Borden was not a man to waste words. But his rage charged the air like an electric current, and Bennett could feel it boiling around him.

The echo of pounding hoofs died in the distance, and Borden's hard breathing was like a whispered warning. He said, "I took you for an honest man, Kell. I credited you with a mistake and took you for an honest man. But you sold me out."

"You're wrong, Ira."

"Wrong?" Borden waved an arm to indicate the vacant bedding ground. His voice was choked with fury and there was madness in his frosty eyes. "My gold is gone, my cattle are gone and my woman's waiting for me in Boston. I was going to her, going to show her what my life in Texas had brought us. Where do I go now, Kell? Admit she was right about a land she always said would only kill us and break us? What do I do, Kell?"

Bennett's mouth tightened. Borden's voice crackled with hate and a note of desperation. It sent a chill of apprehension along Bennett's veins, but he could not spare the time to seek the rancher's understanding. He could not keep his mind off Ada McKittridge, and each passing moment added to his impatience.

He squinted into the growing dusk, scanning the crests of the bare hills. Rusk had not been confident enough of victory to disregard caution. Shortly after the herd was moved, Bennett had spotted the silhouette of a lookout posted atop the hills. The man would stay there as long as he thought it might be necessary to carry a warning to the border gang.

Now the man mounted and rode away, not bothering to conceal himself. He had seen the rebellion in the crew, and his presence was no longer required. What could three men do against Rusk's band?

Bennett had no idea himself, but he could not admit this to Borden. He said, "I'm pulling out, Ira. I aim to make sure my girl is safe and then I'm coming back. I want you to be here. Before I'll let you think I sold you out, I'll tackle Rusk's gang alone. At least, three of us can start a stampede and save part of the herd."

Borden's fists clenched at his sides. "You're a dead man, Kell. I've already asked Cass for his gun, but he refused. With you gone, I'll take it. Keep looking behind you, Kell. I'll be there until I find you."

As Bennett ran toward the picket line to get his dun, Borden's broad back was already turning toward him. Few men could stand up to Ira Borden's determined will without bending under his weight. Cass Bailey was not one of them. Before Bennett could leave the camp, Ira Borden had forced the timid cook to surrender his rifle. And as Bennett swung into saddle he saw the rancher's giant form framed against the firelight, rifle wedged against his shoulder.

Instinctively, Bennett kept moving in the direction he had started. He flung himself across the saddle, and to the ground beyond the horse. In the same instant, the rifle barked. The slug hummed through the air above the saddle, but already Borden was shifting his sight earthward.

Suddenly Bennett was conscious of the gun in his own fist. He had drawn it without thinking, but he was painfully conscious of squeezing the trigger. It was a quick shot, and Bennett cringed as the blast echoed in his ears. Borden's murmur of surprise was barely audible. He staggered, but he righted himself and stayed on his feet. The rifle fell with a clatter. Bennett breathed a ragged sigh, feeling better as Cass Bailey came out of the darkness to grab Borden and help support his weight.

The dun stamped his feet. Bennett grabbed the reins and pulled himself up. He rode close to the horse's neck until he was beyond rifle range. Then he straightened, kicked the dun into a gallop, and rode toward the low hills.

He knew the lay of the land and he had been mentally reviewing it for an hour. As the cattle trails ran, it would take a full day to reach the hideout Bennett had once shared with Toby Rusk and the rest of the border gang. By circling the hills and driving directly northward Bennett had expected to avoid it by many miles.

188

But Toby Rusk had anticipated such a move and had ridden this far to intercept him.

But Rusk was not always so clever. For the most part his thoughts were those of a spiritless man and he exerted himself as little as possible. It was a trait Bennett had spotted long ago and now he gambled that Rusk had remained as lazy as ever. While the Horseshoe was this far away, Rusk would consider the old headquarters a safe hideout. And it was there that Bennett expected to find Ada McKittridge.

He looked at the sky, judging time by the course of the evening star, and he was pressed by anxiety. By following a beeline, riding through timberlands and scaling the ravines, a lone horseman could reach the hidden shack by midnight.

Despite the urgency of his mission, Bennett's thoughts strayed back occasionally to the Horseshoe camp. It was a depressing reminder of failure and his conscience gave him no rest. He had gambled with the crew, too. Once they were paid, he had expected their pride to hold them together until the last bit of hope was gone. Their desertion had disappointed him, but he could not blame them. He could blame only himself for the disaster which had befallen the Horseshoe. Because of this it had taken all his effort to fire at Ira Borden.

But Borden was not dead. Bennett was thankful the man still lived, but it made him uneasy too. As he spurred the dun through the night he cast frequent glances over his shoulder. Each time he half expected to see Ira Borden's gaunt shadow behind him. Borden had said he would be there.

The late July moon was up when Bennett came to the

189

familiar ravine. He rode for a mile along the edge of the rutted hollow which slashed across a corner of open range until it backed into a series of low knolls. From this point it appeared to be clogged to the rim with hawthorn shrubs and red cedar sprouts, and its foreboding shadows were discouraging to a stranger. But Bennett had ridden this way before and he knew it was a deceptive sight. A cleared trail ran through the center of the thicket and there a horseman could conceal himself from the surrounding flats.

He put the dun cautiously over the lip of the ravine and breasted his way into the brush. Branches tore at his worn levis and stung his face. He was hardly conscious of the annoyance. He was within shooting distance of the shack he had once called home, and excitement was flowing through him. He would not allow himself to consider the wisdom of his judgment. This was the only place Rusk could safely hide a woman. Ada had to be here. In another few minutes he would see her again. He could hold her in his arms and know she was safe and he refused to think of anything else.

The dun's instincts were sharper. Suddenly the horse pricked its ears and its muzzle lifted. Bennett's excitement died, smothered by an inkling of danger. A yank of the reins, a quick step, and Bennett was beside the horse's head, stifling the nicker that would give him away. The noise of his own passage had drowned all other sound but now he heard the rhythmic beat of a horse's hoofs. A foot at a time, bending the brush gently aside, Bennett crept forward until he could see the cleared trail through a screen of brush.

He waited breathlessly, knowing he should make a run for the shack before the rider came into sight. But there was danger in either choice, and it took him a moment to decide. He thought of Ada, alone and frightened and uncertain of her fate, and his decision was made. His hand fell away from the dun's muzzle, grabbed for the horn, and the horse plunged toward the trail.

Behind him the hoofbeats quickened. A trapped feeling swept through Bennett and he flung a glance over his shoulder. He swore under his breath and heard an answering curse. That one quick look had verified his suspicions, but he felt no surprise. The moonlight had shown him an angular, dark-skinned face puckered by two deep dimples. The man pressing close to his back was Toby Rusk.

It was a five-hundred-yard race. A short distance ahead, the clearing widened and the shack was nestled beneath the trees on the far side. Bennett nudged the dun with a spur, felt the animal answer with a surge of speed. Another quick glance showed Rusk dropping behind, but the difference in horses was not enough.

Rusk's gun was out now, and he was trying to gauge his aim to the horse's gait. Bennett drew and fired. The bullets were wild, but they caused Rusk's horse to rear and shy off the trail. Rusk lost his grip on the reins, yelled furiously at the horse and tumbled to the ground.

Across the clearing Bennett saw the orange glow of a light. His spurs touched the dun again and the horse bounded toward the shack. Bennett was on his feet before the horse reached a standstill. He opened his mouth to shout encouragement to Ada McKittridge, but the words stuck in his throat.

A shadow glided out of darkness, and a voice asked, "That you, Toby?" And then: "Hell, it's Bennett!"

The guard had stepped out with a rifle held casually in the bend of his arm. Now the weapon snapped in line for a shot.

Eighteen

Even as the man spoke, Bennett heard Toby Rusk's coarse voice screaming curses at his back. With no time to draw his own gun again, Bennett leaped at the guard, his arms clawing for the man's rifle. He got his hands on it, shoved it heavenward. The barrel grew hot in his hands as the weapon exploded. Bennett was like an animal at bay; wildness surged through him. The guard was no match for his savage strength. Bennett tore the rifle from the man's hands, swung it like a club. The gunstock cracked like the slap of a paddle in water, and the guard sank to his knees. He tottered drunkenly a moment and then fell over on his face.

Tossing the rifle aside, Bennett snatched his Colt from the holster. Toby Rusk's bobbing shadow was driving toward him across the clearing. A squeeze of the trigger, a sweep at the hammer, and the gun's roar racketed through the night. Three hasty shots discouraged Toby Rusk. He swung into the bush, ducking out of the moonlight.

Bennett grabbed the unconscious guard beneath the

armpits and shoved his back against the door. It gave beneath his weight and he stumbled inside the musty shack, dragging the guard with him.

The building was a haphazard structure. Chinked logs, with an occasional scrap of plank tacked on, formed the walls. The roof was of matted tree branches, covered with dirt. A rusty iron stove stood in one corner, and up-ended packing crates served as table and chairs.

Bennett's squinted eyes whipped over the crude furnishings. Atop the big crate which served as a table a tallow candle threw flickering shadows across the room. Aside from these things the place appeared empty.

Fear gnawed at his nerves. He rubbed a sleeve across the stubble of his face, tried to swallow against the dryness in his throat. If his hunch about Ada's whereabouts had been wrong his last hope for saving the Horseshoe herd would be gone.

Then he heard the sound. It was the faint hiss of a quick-drawn breath or a muffled sob. His straining ears located the source and he turned swiftly toward the colorless blanket which had been hung from the ceiling near the far corner to form a partition.

He tore the blanket aside with a sweep of his arm. Ada McKittridge sat in a dejected huddle against the wall. Ropes circled her wrists and ankles. A red neck scarf was bound across her mouth. Her golden hair was disarrayed and a ragged tear around the white collar of her gingham dress bared one shoulder and the deep hollow of her breasts.

He removed the gag first, kneeling to gather Ada into his arms. "What have they done to you, Ada?" His

194

voice was choked with rage.

"Nothing yet, Bennett. But I was so afraid. I love you, darling. I love you so very much!"

Some of the fear in him died, but he was keenly aware of Toby Rusk's presence outside. While he worked with the ropes, Ada nestled her head against his shoulder. His hands worked gently over her, rubbing circulation back into her arms and legs.

He was helping Ada to her feet when the first shot ripped through the flimsy walls of the shack. He pushed her back to the packed dirt of the floor and crouched low beside her.

"My friend Toby Rusk," he said grimly. "He's going to try to smoke me out."

Ada shuddered. "When I heard the shots outside, I was afraid those two men—Wally Bryan and Rusk—were arguing over me. The way Rusk looked at me . . . the things he said. I knew he'd come back, too, Bennett and I—I wanted to die."

He gathered up the strands of rope which he had removed from Ada's limbs. His jaws knotted angrily and he slid across the floor toward the groaning guard.

"A nice pair, Ada. Wally Bryan was going to watch Rusk to see that he behaved himself. It's a good thing I know them so well. I knew they wouldn't keep their part of the bargain."

"What bargain, Bennett? All this had something to do with your cattle drive, didn't it? I thought they brought me here just for—for themselves, but it was more, wasn't it?"

He grunted, drawing the ropes tight around the limp, unconscious man he had dumped on the floor near the entrance. Another bullet slammed into the shack, crashing upward through the roof and showering the place with dust. Rusk was shooting wild, but the blast of the gun indicated he was creeping closer all the time. Bennett glanced worriedly at Ada. The shack would be a death trap when Rusk improved his range. He talked to keep Ada's mind off the danger, telling her of the threat Rusk had made and of the Horseshoe's loss.

When he had finished tying the other man, he crawled back to her side, so thrilled with her nearness that the danger was forgotten. She fell back on the hard earth, pulling him down with her. Her lips were warm and pulsating beneath the crush of his mouth, and their desire was a vibrant fire between them.

The jarring report of Toby Rusk's gun drew them apart. The slug drove beneath the skinned-pole door and dug a thin furrow across the earthen floor.

Ada cried out, fearfully. "Will he stay there all night?"

Bennett shook his head. He measured with his eyes the short distance between the bullet trench and Ada. "No. That's one chance I don't aim to take."

Rising, he grabbed at the packing crate table, dumping the candle in the floor. The room was plunged into darkness, but he knew its interior well enough to move about confidently. He shoved the table into a far corner, calling for Ada to follow him. He pushed her down behind the barricade and started away.

"You stay there until I come back. I'm going after Rusk."

"No, Bennett! Please—"

The girl came swiftly to her feet, her arms reaching for him. Bennett's fingers dug into her shoulders, forcing her back. "Don't make me have to slap you,

Ada," he said firmly. *"I'll be back."*

She obeyed meekly. He spent a moment reloading his Colt, then slid quietly against the front wall. He crouched, studying the closed door speculatively, and then sprinted toward it. A bullet crashed through the wall in front of him just as he moved. Pain speared through his face and he paused, blinking stinging tears from his eyes. He touched his cheek hurriedly, feeling the splinters imbedded there, blood already beginning to dribble down, and went on through the door.

He tried to dive for the shadow of a small cedar outside the doorway, but he didn't make it. His boot heel rolled against a stone, and he sprawled awkwardly on his face. At the same moment, Rusk's gun boomed.

Toby Rusk never knew it was an accident. He had been watching the doorway for Bennett's move. His finger was on the rifle trigger and he squeezed it the instant he saw the door swing aside. Moonlight showed him a taut face with a smear of blood on it. Bennett had fallen heavily, and Rusk thought he was dead.

Bennett had bunched his muscles to spring for cover when he saw Rusk step into the open. He tensed, wondering at the bold move, but Rusk's confident manner gave him a hint of the man's thoughts. The brawny raider came slowly out of the shadows thirty yards away. His head was pushed forward on his short neck and his rifle was braced against his shoulder. There was no stealth in Rusk's stride, and he seemed confident of himself as he came steadily toward Bennett Kell, wanting to make sure of his marksmanship.

Bennett's hat was mashed against the side of his head, but he could see Rusk clearly under the edge of the brim. He held his breath, counting the steps, and the gun in his outstretched hand raised gradually to hold Rusk in its sights.

Rusk must have seen the slight movement. His arm went rigid, and Bennett fired. A black smudge appeared between Rusk's eyes and his head rocked back between his shoulders. The impact of the bullet ripped the rifle barrel just enough to send Rusk's shot over Bennett's head. Afterward, Rusk kept leaning backward until he hit the ground. A puff of dust floated up around him, but Rusk did not move.

Bennett climbed wearily to his feet. Ada came to him the moment his shadow filled the doorway, hugging him with relief. She drew away with a gasp when she noticed the blood on his cheek. He told her that the wound was only splinter scratches.

She reached for his arms again but he held her away from him. "I want you to take the lookout's horse and ride out of here, Ada," he said urgently. "From here on the trail ought to be safe if you keep moving. At least you'll be safer than you will with me. I'll tell you how to find your way while we're looking for the horse."

He took her by the hand, but Ada held back. "You're going to send me back to Kansas City alone, Bennett? I won't go. I've found you again, and I'm never going anywhere unless you go with me."

He shook his head irritably. "Ada, the bargain I made with your uncle has got to be kept or I'll never feel like much of a man. When I go to Kansas City I want to be driving cattle in front of me."

Ada pulled her hand free of his grasp. "You're acting like a fool, Bennett. The cattle are gone and your men

198

have deserted you. You can't whip the rest of that gang by yourself."

"I'll find a way." His voice was a solemn whisper. "Ira Borden put a lot of trust in me and he thinks I sold him out. If he goes on thinking that and telling folks that, I might as well have stayed with the border gangs. I've got to go back, Ada. If worst comes to worst, I'll make a deal with Nelse Garwood and split the herd with him. But Ira Borden's going to drive some of those cows to the loading pens."

His hand found her arm again and this time the grip was tighter. He went out of the cabin that way, forcing her to follow, but he did not dare look back at her until he had found the horse. After he helped her into the saddle, he pulled her head down close to his and looked into her face. He ran his fingertips gently across the tears of her heavy lashes and kissed her quickly.

"Ride fast, Ada, and you'll be home shortly after daybreak. I've put Rusk's rifle in the saddle boot. If anybody tries to stop you, use it."

She choked back the tears. "When will I see you, Bennett?"

"Maybe in two days, maybe later. But don't worry, Ada. Nothing can keep me away from you—nothing."

She lifted the reins and went away at a gallop, waving to him until the darkness swallowed her. Bennett stared after her, his heart heavy. He must be a fool to pursue a lost cause while the woman he loved rode away alone on a dangerous trail. He must be an even greater fool, he reflected as he mounted the dun, to ride back and face the fury of Ira Borden.

But it was a thing Bennett had to do.

It took him more time to return to the Horseshoe camp than it had to reach the hideout shack, but he arrived long before daylight. Atop one of the bald hills, he rested the dun. He sat for a while surveying the camp, a dark, brooding man with a tired slump to his shoulders and a hard set to his face.

Behind the dun was another horse, held in tow with a lead rope. The extra mount had delayed him but he felt it would prove worth the trouble. Across the saddle of the second horse lay a dead man. At first Bennett had considered staying in the ravine long enough to bury Toby Rusk's body, but it occurred to him that the corpse might help him prove his honesty to Ira Borden. And later, if he could find help, Rusk's body would serve as an advantage against Wally Bryan.

A few miles away, Bryan would be camped with the rest of the border gang. Before daylight, Bennett hoped to drive the horse and its grim burden that way. It would be a warning to Wally Bryan and he hoped, a shock to the ruffians who had accepted Toby Rusk as their leader. The sight of death could weaken a man's will for battle. And when Bennett found a way to strike at them he wanted them to remember Toby Rusk.

But Ira Borden came first. Bennett had told the rancher about Rusk many times and he had mentioned the bullet scars in the rider's swarthy cheeks. One look at the still form should convince Borden that Bennett's break with the border gang was final.

Keeping the horses to a fast walk, Bennett came down from the hills and slowly approached the Horseshoe camp. His eyes were cautious and alert, sweeping over the dark land in search of danger signals. The short hairs at the back of his neck rose in apprehension. He circled wide around the low-burning fire, setting his course for the remuda. Out of habit, he removed his black Stetson and hung it on the horn as he came within shooting range.

A voice reached out at him from amid the horses stamping along the picket lines. "You just saved your life, Bennett. You told us to shoot anything we saw wearing a hat, and I sure had a steady bead on you."

Bennett was too startled to move. A lump rose in his throat, and he swallowed twice before he found his voice. Then: "That you, Bert?"

"The same," Bert Roscoe said. He stepped out from the horses, a broad grin on his face. "Got here two hours ago. Found Cass here by hisself, and the Old Man out riding the hills and calling down hellfire and damnation on your head. Me and Zumbro rode out and convinced him he ought to let things simmer until he found out exactly what you aimed to do. He seemed plumb tickled to see us."

"I'm obliged to you, Bert," Bennett said, dismounting. The smile on his face warmed his eyes and he slapped Bert Roscoe's shoulder gratefully. Briefly, he told Roscoe about Toby Rusk and the reason for bringing the body with him.

"Then we got no reason for backing up from that bunch now," Roscoe said. "Your girl's safe and they've got nothing to hold over our heads."

"That's right. How many of the crew came back with you?"

Bert Roscoe grinned. He turned toward the fire and raised his voice in a piercing rebel yell. Bennett's heart jumped hopefully when he heard the stir of many booted feet. Curses drifted through the air in a variety of tones, and presently he saw a mass of familiar shadows.

"Come on," Roscoe said, "and we'll have roll call."

As Bennett turned he came face to face with Ira Borden. His body went rigid as he looked for the signs of fury he had learned so well—the tight lips, the throbbing vein at the temple.

But Ira Borden appeared completely relaxed. He stood with one foot set slightly in front of the other, resting his weight on his right leg. Through a tear in the levis covering the other leg, Bennett saw the outline of a white bandage.

"I'm sorry about that, Ira," he said quietly, dropping his gaze toward the injured leg.

"It was a fair exchange. I was shooting at you. Maybe I made a mistake. We'll see."

Borden's words were curt, spoken without any show of emotion. He turned and a muscle twitched across his jawbone. But he refused to limp. Over his shoulder he said, "In case I was right about you, Kell, we'll settle it later. Right now I reckon there's some friends of yours waiting."

They were all there, looking ashamed at first, and then straightening with pride. Ben Lufton's soft drawl broke through the din of voices. He said, "You knowed we'd be back, Bennett, or you'd have killed somebody over that gold. We got to talking among ourselves and nobody knowed exactly why we were running out, seeing as how all the promises to us have been kept. So we swapped ends of the horses. We just lost one war and damned if we aim to surrender so easy again."

Strained laughter ran through the crowd, and Bennett was aware of Bonnie Gray's throaty voice. He saw her standing with Wade Zumbro near the fire. His eyes met hers and she winked at him. There was little doubt in his mind that she had been a strong influence in the decision to return.

Ira Borden remained silent until the handshakes were over and Bennett had spoken a word of thanks to each man. He had stood at Bennett's side, a strange patience and restraint in his manner.

Finally he said, "You're back, Kell. I understand your woman is safe. What do you plan to do now?"

"I figure to get your cattle back."

"When?" Borden's voice crackled and a fiery light danced in his eyes.

"A few miles back, I rode across some high ground and I spotted their fire," Bennett said. "They're not more than four-five miles from here, Ira. We ought to hit them before daylight."

Borden looked at the sky. "That gives us two hours."

"That's time enough." Bennett turned his attention to the waiting crew. "You leather-pushers can load your guns and saddle your horses. We're ready for that fight I've been telling you about."

Nineteen

There was urgency in Bennett's voice and it brought a sparkle to the eyes of the men who heard it. It flickered briefly in most of them and died, and a deep silence held them. Men would die this night. The thought was among them, and they paused to reflect, to recall a fond memory or feel their regrets.

Bennett did not hurry them. His own mind ran along with theirs. He thought of Ada McKittridge, and of the life he hoped to build with her. Miles away, she was riding through the night alone, perhaps afraid, perhaps in danger.

A match flared at the back of the crowd. The fragrance of tobacco smoke drifted through the air and Bennett could sense the quick passing of the lull.

Wade Zumbro stepped aside and spoke softly to Bonnie Gray. He took her in his arms and kissed her, wheeling abruptly to head for the horses. The others followed, hands dropping to adjust their holsters. Bennett reached out and grabbed Cass Bailey's arm as the cook went by, instructing him to remain at the wagons with Bonnie Gray. Then he quickened his pace to overtake the crew.

Ira Borden had not waited. His saddle was on a strong gray horse, and the rancher stood with his hand clamped impatiently on the horn. But he said nothing. As the men began cutting out their horses, Borden's eyes turned northward, in the direction where he had last seen his herd.

Bennett saddled the big sorrel he rode when the dun needed rest. He reached a foot for the stirrup, missed by an inch, and tottered uncertainly as he lost his balance.

"You're dead on your feet, Kell," Ira Borden said quietly. "You've been in the saddle all night. It's asking a lot for you to keep going."

Bennett raised his gaze to the rancher's face. He was amazed at the kindness in Borden's voice, but he hid it under a tight smile. "I may be tuckered, Ira, but this is something that I have to do."

Borden's expression remained unchanged. He looked beyond Bennett, saw men swinging to saddle, and climbed aboard his own horse. He said, "You want to talk here or wait until we get there, Kell?"

"We'll wait. I want to see if Wally Bryan is set up for us. Before I left their hideout I loosened the ropes some on that guard. Didn't want him to starve to death in case nobody looked for him. Maybe he got back and warned them."

Borden snorted. "Sometimes you're soft to a fault, Kell."

Bennett picked up the lead rope of the horse which

205

carried Toby Rusk's body, mounted with a tired grunt. "Rusk said the same thing once, Ira. Now look where he is."

Bennett's voice was harsh and impatient. He was tired of waiting, tired of the everlasting tension that kept his stomach muscles aquiver. Now he was only a hard day's ride from Kansas City, and the nearness of his goal was like an enticing prize dangling beyond a huge abyss. He wanted to make the final leap.

He looked behind him, found the crew ready and shot spurs to his horse. Across the strip of flatland, cornering around the rolling hills, Bennett led the Horseshoe crew at a gallop. Behind him, the rattle of Toby Rusk's jostling spurs was a constant reminder that death was a grim partner who rode with him.

High in the sky, the sliver of silver moon was paling under a misty haze and tufts of gray clouds began to show here and there. Bennett rode high in the stirrups, sighting the land ahead as he tried to recall the exact location of the campfire he had seen earlier. They had little time to spare before daylight, and he was trying to slash through the circle which had to be followed to take the herd around the hills.

Ira Borden kept pace with Bennett's mount, his stirrups bouncing rhythmically a yard away. Borden's features were locked in a tight visage. His lips were clamped tight, his eyes glazed with preoccupation, and his hand went often to the cedar-butted Colt which Bennett passed across to him as they left the wagons. He was going after his cattle and the devil himself could not stop him.

In less than an hour, the glow of the border gang's

fire showed like a red halo against the earth. Bennett slowed his horse, waved the others into a line beside him. He led them to a point within five hundred yards of the bedded herd and dismounted, calling the crew in close around him.

He said quietly, "We walk in from here. Move as fast as you can, but don't budge until you're sure nobody is going to spot you. First we'll try to get the nighthawks out of our way. There'll probably be upwards of a dozen of them. They've got plenty of men and they'll want plenty guarding that herd. Try to slip in among the cattle, but don't start them milling. Every time a rider passes you, drag him out of the saddle and lay your gun against his head. Throw his gun away, and use his saddle rope to tie him up if you get a chance. Later, I'll—"

"You're wasting time, Kell," Ira Borden cut in sharply. The rancher pushed to the front of the circle. He set a hand on the butt of his gun and shook his head irritably. "That way we run the risk of a slip-up we can't afford. One wrong move at the nighthawks and they'll know we're there. If somebody raises a shout we won't stand a prayer. We'll go straight to them. We'll empty our guns at the men at the fire, and take the cattle guards as we come to them. We'll do better if we surprise them."

Bennett straightened. His dark eyes met the cold gray of Borden's glance. "We settled this once, Ira. I boss these men. You're forgetting there'll be eighteen-nineteen guns firing back at us the minute they get over their surprise. If I can get those cattle back without killing anybody, that's the way I want to do it."

207

"They deserve killing," Borden snapped fiercely.

Bennett's mouth became a thin line against his dark face. He gestured at the men beside him. "These, too?"

Borden's hard glance dropped to the ground. He stared at the toes of his scuffed boots, hitched at his heavy gunbelt, and strode away without replying.

"We'll do it the way I said," Bennett continued. "After you get rid of the guards, circle around to the north side of their campfire. I'll be waiting there. Nobody fires a shot unless I holler for it."

One at a time the men drifted into the darkness. Ira Borden started with them, turning after a few feet to stare back at Bennett Kell. Bennett tensed, half-expecting Borden to go charging toward the fire with his gun roaring. Then the rancher went on toward the herd.

Shadows bobbed in the early morning darkness. Bennett looked at the sky and was grateful for nature's help. Lead-gray clouds had drifted in from the southwest, growing constantly in size until the moon was blotted from sight. The stretch of flatland was dotted with brush patches, and the Horseshoe used them to shield their advance.

Bennett went with them, deciding on a course which would take him far to the right of the cattle. He went a hundred yards in a stooped, sprinting crouch. He came to the edge of a head-high cutbank and slid into its depths. The eroded trench curved to pass within thirty paces of the campfire, and as he hurried along he could hear the murmur of voices. Dropping to his stomach as the gully grew shallow, he wriggled forward until he was only a few paces from the outer fringes of the sleeping cattle.

A steer swung its head and looked at him curiously. Bennett inched cautiously forward, humming softly under his breath, and the steer did not rise. Then he was lying in the grass among the herd, feeling the animal heat from their bodies and smelling the rancid odor of dust-coated hides.

His searching eyes could find no sign of another human being, but he could feel the presence of others around him. The cattle could sense the presence of intruders, too, and a current of excitement ran through the herd. First came a restless switching of tails and a tossing of long-horned heads. Then a plaintive bawl and a suspicious animal clambered to its feet.

Bennett saw the silhouette of a slow-moving rider circling toward him. He hunkered among the bodies of the cattle, his nerves tingling with the fear of discovery. The rider came closer, stopped his mount and rose in the stirrups. His face was turned away from Bennett as he murmured, "I wonder what—" and stopped in amazement as a firm grip tugged at his arm.

This was the dangerous moment, and Bennett yanked viciously at the man's arm, slashing at him with his gun the instant the rider tottered sideways in the saddle. A faint groan came from the rider and his feet came free of the stirrups. Bennett eased him gently to the ground. Afterward, he took the man's rifle from the saddle boot, removed the holstered gun and tossed both of them into the darkness beyond. By the time he had used the saddle rope to bind the man's arms and legs, Bennett was panting and his legs were shaking with fatigue.

It was energy he could not afford, but he had been unwilling to send the Horseshoe crew on such a perilous assignment without having a part of it. But his own interest lay at the fire. That was where he would find Wally Bryan, and that was where the battle would be won or lost.

Crawling on hands and knees, Bennett started back the way he had come. He ducked among the cattle again as another horseman came into view a short distance farther on. And while he watched, the rider abruptly disappeared from sight, leaving an empty saddle. Bennett darted toward the spot, ready to lend a hand. But his help was not needed. He raised his head far enough to be recognized, said in a whisper, "Good, work, Shad. Keep at it. You can mount that horse now. The guard up ahead will figure you're his pard."

Shad Miller's white teeth flashed in a grin, and the cotton-haired youngster moved on without speaking. The plan was working. All around the herd the men of the Horseshoe were swinging their guns, dragging stunned riders to the ground. As he went away from the bedding ground, Bennett looked frequently over his shoulder. He could see furtive movements here and there, but so far there had been no cry of alarm. Ira Borden had not needed to worry about a surprise attack, Bennett reflected. With Ada McKittridge as a hostage, the border gang had been confident of their safety.

It seemed like miles back to the horses, and Bennett began to worry about dwindling time. His uneasy glances at the sky showed him a faint blue line near the eastern horizon and nervousness gripped him. Darkness was his greatest ally.

The horses stood with trailing reins, accustomed to

this patient waiting. Only one of them stamped its feet fretfully as Bennett approached. It was the horse he had led behind his own, not yet accustomed to the smell of death on its back.

Catching the tie rope, he freed the horse and started again toward the raiders' camp. Excitement was a hot wire through his body, and it drove the fatigue out of him. He paused frequently, peering through the gloom at the dark bulk of the herd. From the beginning he had lived with a constant fear that a gun would blast in the night, and that a pitched battle would begin.

The fear was still with him. It was a clammy sweat over his body and haste into his steps. He swung wide around the distant fire, led the horse into the cutbank on the north. Afterward, he crept cautiously forward until he could hear the simmer of burning logs and the hum of voices from the camp.

Ira Borden rose from the shadows of the gulley. He crawled to Bennett's side and squatted at his heels. "The boys are all here. I've got them strung out along the cutbank. When do we open fire?"

Removing his hat, Bennett eased his head above the rim of the gully and looked at the night camp. Two men sat with their backs toward him. Facing them across the fire, his thin face lighted by flickering flames, was Wally Bryan. Farther on Bennett counted the bulging blanket rolls where five other raiders were asleep.

"Holler when you're ready," Borden said gruffly.

"I'll do that, Ira. But be sure you keep these men under cover until I yell. They'll stay alive longer that way. First, I aim to go in alone."

A grunt of disgust came from Borden. He started to

say something, but Bennett moved before the rancher could speak. He took the horse with him, creeping farther along the dry ditch. Curious glances swung his way as he passed members of the Horseshoe crew.

He reached the shallow end and led the horse out on the flat. He glanced worriedly at the eastern horizon, frowning at the first gray fingers of dawn reaching into the sky. He took a deep breath, measuring the distance to the campfire. Then he walked boldly forward. His fingers were trembling as he worked with the horse's reins, looping them around the horn. His arms rubbed against Toby Rusk's cold back and the feel of death made his stomach queasy.

When he was less than fifty feet away, he slapped the horse gently on the rump and dropped to the ground. The tied reins kept the horse moving. It was almost at the edge of the firelight before the crunch of a hoof announced its coming. A startled curse, the hiss of guns being drawn and the trio at the fire wheeled to stare at the tired bronc. Then there was silence until one of them finally edged out to grab at the bridle.

"My God!" a man said hoarsely. "There's a dead man on the saddle!" And then the voice rose to a high pitch, shouting, "Hell, it's Toby Rusk. Somebody's killed Toby Rusk, Wally!"

Bennett had been on his feet since the first startled curse. While their attention was distracted, he managed to come closer without being heard. Now he stepped into the open. The raiders had begun to fumble with the ropes which bound Rusk's body to the saddle, and their guns were holstered.

Bennett's own hands hung limply at his sides. He

knew Wally Bryan's gun speed, and he did not want to make the man draw. While he kept his hands empty he would have a chance to talk.

"You'll all end up across a saddle if you reach for a gun," he said flatly. "There's a ring of Texans around you, Wally. We've come for our cows and we don't want to kill anybody."

Twenty

There was an instant of frozen stillness while men beyond astonishment groped for their reasoning powers. They had believed Toby Rusk too tough to kill, too clever to fail; and Bennett Kell, they thought, had been hopelessly beaten, held at bay by an ultimatum he could not afford to challenge.

Yet Rusk was dead, and Bennett Kell stood defiantly before them. Firelight cast an eerie glow across the pallid, blood-crusted features of the lifeless thing which had once been Toby Rusk. The drooping horse stamped and shied and tossed its head, asking to be rid of the gruesome burden.

Bennett Kell was struck by the savagery of this scene of his own creation, and for an instant he was ashamed and fearful. In the past few hours he had become a stranger to himself, a man who rode the hills with a dead man for company, and seized upon a corpse as an instrument of battle!

He had only seconds to face his misgivings and thrust them aside. It was done while stunned faces turned his way, and while shaken, unnerved men gathered their wits. He kept his eyes on Wally Bryan's sharp-boned face. All the danger rested with the thin, handsome gunman.

Shock continued to hold the raiders. Those in their beds sprang to their feet, murmured in amazement, and drifted in beside the fire. Their glances went first to the horse, and the sight of the corpse snapped them awake. The presence of Bennett Kell told them the story, and they ranged themselves behind Wally Bryan—waiting.

Four of the men had once worked with Bennett. They had accepted his authority, obeyed his orders, and he gambled that habit would guide them. He took three steps forward, ignoring Wally Bryan momentarily. He said sharply, "Cliff, Frank, Dave . . . Johnny! Be smart and shuck off your guns. Rusk was all you had to bank on, and he's dead! I'm not bluffing. I've got men scattered along the cutbank over there."

Wally Bryan made a half-turn in his quick, effortless way. He ordered them to stand as they were, but his words were too late.

Bennett breathed easier as a gunbelt plopped into the dirt. Another followed, and then there was a glistening pile of them. When it was over, only Wally Bryan still wore his gun.

A life at the poker tables had left its mark on Wally Bryan. It was his nature to buck uneven odds. And when the odds were too great, he counted on his gun speed to make them even.

"Well the damn fools fell for it," he said. "They forget we've got a dozen men with the cattle. You fire a shot, Bennett, and we'll eat that handful of Texans for breakfast."

"We took care of the nighthawks, Wally. This thing will be settled before they get over the lumps we put on their heads. Throw in your gun. Ira Borden's waiting to move his cattle away from here."

Firelight glistened on Wally Bryan's slick black hair as he shook his head slowly from side to side. His slender shoulders squared and pinpoints of light danced in his eyes. The supple fingers of his right hand flexed slightly.

"You never knew about Toby Rusk and me," Wally Bryan murmured through tight lips. "Toby kept a man from sticking a knife in my back one night in a poker game. Because of that I never crossed him. It kept me from taking over this gang the day you left. Now I can do it, Bennett. I can square the account for Toby and have my own way."

"You can't win, Wally."

"It's a big pot, Bennett—worth the gamble." He gestured at the cowed, silent group a short distance away. "They thought they had lost their leader, so they quit. Your Texas crew will be the same way without you. They won't fight."

Wally Bryan's features froze into a bland expression. The challenge had come in the same silken tones Wally Bryan used to greet a woman.

Behind Bennett, eight men had their guns trained on the border gang's camp. He could raise his voice and those guns would speak, but they could not save him. Wally Bryan was as tense and dangerous as a bent bow, and a single sound would set him off. He would die in the end, but Bennett Kell would die first.

Bennett's breath swelled his chest and he seemed unable to let it go. He felt the moistness of his palms

216

and the leap of his heart, but he did not bother to weigh his chances. He had no choice, and now it seemed that his life had been directed toward this moment since the first time he came to Missouri.

"Waiting," Wally Bryan said flatly.

A single word, but it meant one of them must die. Bennett Kell knew it, and as the time ran out for them, he was suddenly aware that the blast of a gun would give him little satisfaction. He needed something more, a final expression of the revulsion within him. Ira Borden had found an answer to this, and now Bennett used it. He scraped his tongue around inside his dry mouth and spat abruptly at Wally Bryan's chest.

Wally Bryan recoiled as though slapped in the face. His dark eyes flitted to the damp spot on his black broadcloth shirt, and he breathed a bewildered curse. And then a long-fingered hand was clawing for the shiny Colt.

Down and up, Wally's hand moved in flawless motion. Bennett could not match that deadly speed. He had known this from the start and his reflexes were keyed for defense.

With the first hint of motion, he twisted aside. Flame and lead poured from Wally Bryan's Colt. A shocking force smashed at Bennett's left shoulder, knocking him off balance. Searing, nauseating pain ripped through his torso as he dropped to one knee, bracing himself on the ground.

His mind was still clear and his gun was free. Wally Bryan's muscles were still working on impulse, and the roar of a second shot blended with the echo of the first. The bullet went wild, cutting the air where Bennett had stood before.

217

The Colt bucked in Bennett's fist. Wally Bryan's shirt front fluttered briefly, as though touched by wind. Then blood spurted from the hole over his heart and he pitched forward on his face.

Bennett stayed where he was, an arm braced across his knee. His shirt was damp with his own blood, and it seemed that the pain Wade Zumbro's spurs had put in the shoulder had never left him. His eyes felt heavy and his head was filled with buzzing noises.

A man at the fire knelt beside Wally Bryan's body, felt for a pulse. He shook his head slowly at the others and got back to his feet.

"Well, what about it?" Bennett asked. His voice was hoarse, impatient. "Who wants to take this thing up?"

Johnny English, one of the men who had known the gang under Bennett's leadership, spoke for all of them. He turned his hands up in defeat. "It's all over, Bennett. Me, I figure I'll ride out to California. A man might make a start there."

The others began looking around for their belongings, and Bennett could not stifle the sense of pity he felt for the aimless life they had made for themselves. He was grateful that he was not still among them.

With supreme effort, he forced himself to stand. The ground rocked under his feet and the buzzing noises in his head grew louder. Suddenly the pounding in his ears sounded like the distant rumble of thunder and he rubbed a hand fiercely across his eyes, trying to hold his senses.

Slowly he turned toward the cutbank to call the Horseshoe crew. He blinked at the line of men behind him. Ira Borden stood not ten feet away, a stone-faced statue in the eerie gray light of dawn. Ranged around

218

him with guns in their hands were the others of the drive. They had been there since the shooting ended.

"We better move the herd now, Ira," Bennett said.

Borden nodded. There was no handshake, no word of thanks from him. He paid a man to do a job, and Bennett Kell had done a job.

He said, "I've sent Clay Macklin to tell Cass and the girl to catch up. You can wait here for them, Kell. A day in the wagon will do you good. How bad's that shoulder?"

"No bones broken. In the front and out the back. Cass would say. I'll ask him to patch it up."

"You better sit down before you fall down," Borden grunted, and turned away.

Bennett started to ease himself to the ground. He bent only a knee, but his whole body went limp. His vision clouded and the earth tilted up to meet him.

Big Jim McKittridge's heavy-jowled face held a pinkish glow. He stood with his hands clasped behind him and rocked gently on his heels while his glance swept along the row of new loading pens strung out beside the railroad track. The pens were filling with cattle and McKittridge was keeping an eye on the men who were tallying the Horseshoe herd.

Bennett Kell pulled his dun away from the mass of bawling animals and started toward the railroad man. McKittridge looked even bigger and more prosperous than Bennett remembered him, and the fragrance of the man's cigar was a pleasant smell over the stench of the cattle.

Seeing him so preoccupied Bennett was not certain

219

of the reception he would receive. He had been in doubt ever since he had learned McKittridge and a posse of townsmen had ridden out to greet the herd two days ago. At that time, Bennett was riding the supply wagon, still unconscious from exhaustion and the wound from Wally Bryan's bullet.

Cass Bailey had told Bennett of the man's visit. Ada had arrived safely in Kansas City, but McKittridge was so upset by her experience that he had gathered a posse and ridden out to settle a score with the border gang himself. As soon as he learned the leaderless, disorganized band had scattered without further trouble, McKittridge had turned and ridden back to Kansas City, without troubling to rouse Bennett or to leave a message for him.

A voice rose above the milling cattle to interrupt Bennett's thoughts. Shad Miller rode up beside him, slanting the brim of his hat to block the mid-afternoon sun.

"Just wanted to tell you," Shad grinned, "not to run off anywhere until next week. I'm aiming to have me a real party on my birthday and I want to buy you a drink."

Bennett smiled and shook his head. "You stay away from liquor and wild women, Shad. Do that and get a good night's sleep once in a while and you might get full grown yet."

Shad Miller's eyes twinkled with anticipation. "I'll do that, Bennett. After what I've been through the last month, you can bet I'll do just that!"

He backed his horse away, and a loud laugh floated behind him. The smile faded from Bennett's face as he went to meet McKittridge. He stepped down stiffly, grimacing as he jostled the sling which held his left arm.

"Howdy, Mr. McKittridge," he said simply. "I'm back."

"And I'm delighted to see you, Kell!" McKittridge's face wrinkled with his broad smile and he shook Bennett's hand vigorously. "Indeed, you're one man I'm delighted to see."

"I wondered. I was with the herd when you rode out to it."

The coolness of Bennett's voice caused McKittridge to frown. "I didn't mean any slight, Bennett. The men told me something of the hell you'd been through, and I thought it would be cruel to cheat you of your rest. So I didn't wake you. And there wasn't time to wait until you woke of your own accord. Ada was quite disturbed, and she had my promise that I would come back and tell her the minute I knew you were safe."

McKittridge took Bennett's arm, guiding him a few feet away from Ira Borden who had been standing at the railroader's side.

"I'm proud of you, Kell," he said firmly. "The minute I saw you, I knew you were the kind who takes the world by the horns and shakes it until it takes the right shape. I've made a place for you, my boy. Now that we're into Abilene, I want you to get out there. You'll be in complete charge of cattle inspections and shipping if things work as they should."

Bennett frowned. "What's this Abilene?"

McKittridge explained. "The railroad has moved well into Kansas. We've decided to make Abilene our main cattle station. There's a trail which leads due north out of Texas, they tell me. The town will boom and so will the cattle lands. It'll be beyond the Missouri farmers and the gangs that have grown around them. There'll be no more border raids when we start shipping from there."

Bennett said nothing. A weary sigh escaped his lips and he shook his head, thinking back to the fight with Zumbro, to the humiliation which had been forced upon Farley Jones. He thought of the sleepless nights and dreary days and all the tensions which had sprung from the temptation of Ira Borden's gold and Bonnie Gray's presence.

McKittridge touched his shoulder. "You seem troubled, Kell. You have no cause to be. You've got every reason to celebrate."

"Have I, Mr. McKittridge? From what you say, they'll be shipping out of Abilene town in a month or two." Bennett raised his glance to study the weary riders who were closing the last chute gates and cantering toward them. "I was thinking we didn't accomplish much to brag about. We could have waited a spell and made this drive to Abilene without asking so much of everybody. This way it seems like a hell of a waste."

McKittridge puffed at his cigar. He gave Bennett a solemn look and tilted his head toward the approaching riders. "Take a look at your crew, and think about it some more. They're a different sort from those you used to ride with. It couldn't have been a waste, Kell."

The crew was there. They drew to a halt in a shower of dust, and Bennett looked up at them. Old Ben Lufton touched a finger to his hat in quiet salute.

"I'm off for Texas, Bennett," the wrangler drawled softly. "My woman ain't seen real money in a coon's age, and she'll be fretting for a look. When I get back

222

home I'll be telling folks about Bennett Kell and this ride to Missouri."

"You do that, Ben. I'll be obliged."

Bennett spoke in unashamed frankness. Many of the crew would be in Texas before him, and they would make his own return much easier. He wanted the folks at home to know that he had been true to a trust, true to a promise. When Texans heard of the drive to Missouri, they would know there was a turning point for a man headed wrong when he turned with a will that could leave no doubt.

"I'll tell them," Ben Lufton said, and turned his horse. Cass Bailey, looking awkward astride a long-legged bay, waved an arm and turned with him. The others said their farewells, some turning south and some heading toward the terraced slope where Kansas City throbbed with excitement.

Bennett watched them go, his thoughts running back over Big Jim McKittridge's words. The drive to Missouri had not saved the state of Texas: the trail to Abilene would do that. But perhaps it had done as much. It had given men new faith and hope and a spirit that would inspire others in all the battles yet to come before this sprawling new land was peacefully settled. Even Bonnie Gray had changed, aware at last of a woman's reward for offering strength and encouragement to the man she loved. She rode toward town at Wade Zumbro's side, and she would stay there until they prospered together, no longer grabbing for the quick riches that came at the cost of pride and respect.

McKittridge had been right, Bennett thought as the crew faded from sight. He had not wasted himself.

"About that job," McKittridge began anew. "I

223

promised you I'd—".

Bennett raised a hand to stop him. "All I want is wages and a wife, Mr. McKittridge. I've got my place on the Brazos, and it needs looking after."

A flush of color swept through McKittridge's round cheeks. He stared at Bennett and rocked speculatively on his heels. At last he shrugged, turning his hands up in a gesture of defeat.

"Ada's waiting at the hotel. You're a fool, man, but you seem to be the kind of fool who will make my niece happy. Go to her!"

Smiling, Bennett reached for the saddle horn. He hesitated as Ira Borden called his name.

"Thanks!" Borden said. It was a big word, from Ira Borden. Except for his money, he had little for which to thank this demanding land which had cost him a son, cost him a wife, and hardened him to a point that made others uncomfortable in his presence.

But Borden was smiling now, thinking of a reunion in Boston; and in this he and Bennett were kindred souls.

Ada McKittridge was only a few blocks away. A wave of his hand, and Bennett Kell was riding toward her, remembering the promise of those brief moments together at Toby Rusk's hideout shack. While Borden and McKittridge completed their business transactions, Bennett and Ada would have an hour alone to dream of their future.

This time, there would be no threat of gunfire to distract them.